Susan Wicks

LITTLE THING

faber and faber
LONDON · BOSTON

First published in 1998
by Faber and Faber Limited
3 Queen Square London WC1N 3AU

Photoset by Avon Dataset Ltd, Bidford on Avon, Warwickshire
Printed in England by Clays Ltd, St Ives plc

© Susan Wicks, 1998

Susan Wicks is hereby identified as author of this work in accordance with
Section 77 of the Copyright, Designs and Patents Act 1988

A CIP record for this book
is available from the British Library

ISBN 0-571-19344-7

I would like to thank the MacDowell Colony and
Djerassi Resident Artists Program, who gave me the time and space I
needed to write the first draft of this book.   SW

2 4 6 8 10 9 7 5 3 1

1

NONE OF IT MATTERS now I have the child. For the moment she is sleeping, one cheek pressed against the mattress, her skin slightly pink from the pressure, one hand uncurling on air, the other thumb just slipped from her mouth. She is too hot, little wisps of hair sticking to her nape in a whorled pattern like shells or fingerprints, damp with sweat, almost dark. I creep to the cot, the floorboards creaking under my bare feet, and pull back the blanket. She doesn't wake. I tiptoe to the open window and kneel down on the wide stone sill.

The lane is still full of mist. Up the hill the trees meet in grey shapes, barely distinguishable in their haze of filtered sunlight. In the field the cows stand knee-deep, pause in their munching to stare at me, their slow heads turning one by one in my direction until I feel pinned against stone. I pull back into the room. As I move a pale ribbon of sunlight falls across the floor, unrolling towards the empty bed.

And you have gone now. You would be proud of me. You would be proud of her, though she isn't at all like you. She is too perfect to be like either of us.

I would like to send you this, this brief picture, our child asleep in her cot. The shape of her small body that rises and falls as she breathes. The painted wooden bars already scarred with toothmarks about halfway up, where she pulls herself to her feet to look through. This old stone cottage with its bare floors, eaten away in places by woodworm or just old age, the huge oak beams of the downstairs ceiling blackened by the smoke of centuries. The rumpled sheets still trailing from my bed. This stripe of raw sun. I move back to the window and the patch of light on the floor flickers and goes out as I block it with my body. In her cot our child stirs and I hear the sound of sucking as the thumb finds its way back. The lush grass down there underneath me is colourless through the bright mist. It's going to be even hotter than it was yesterday. I squint and make out a duck – the she-duck standing at the edge of the small pond, her head on one side, preening. She waddles towards me across the patch of grass, as if she sensed food. And now the drake is there too, appearing round the corner as if from nowhere, a darker shadow against her white. 'Go away. I've nothing to give you.' I lean from the window and gesticulate. 'Nothing. *Rien*. Look.' I show them my empty hands, the sun red in the interstices of my fingers. Almost in unison they open their big beaks and start to quack.

I tread carefully between the half-packed cardboard boxes that litter the upstairs landing and find my way downstairs. The sitting-room is scarcely any better, the sofa sagging under its pile of books and toys, a white wicker armchair draped with hastily folded clothes, some of them already outgrown. And even in the heat of summer the same smell over it all, last year's smell of soot and woodsmoke from the cast-iron stove, the cold damp months we have lived through still clinging in the fibres, even in this heat.

Before she wakes I must do all I can. I unlock the kitchen door and go round to the washing-line. But the stuff I pegged out yesterday evening has got damp again from the dew and mist. It will be another few hours yet before I can use it or fold it up with the rest. A shirt flaps in my face, cool, smelling of grass. A small voice somewhere in the bedroom above me starts to rise in protest, then subsides again into a murmur. I pick up the laundry basket and clutch it to my hip.

But as I turn to go back inside, the ducks come at me from behind, attacking me with a violence that seems hungry rather than playful, pecking at the backs of my legs. I hear myself shriek with the surprise. 'Get off me! *Mais qu'est-ce qui vous prend*? Ridiculous birds.' I run towards the door and they follow me in a series of little rushes. I escape through the open door and slam it shut against them. My head and neck prickle with sweat. I put down the basket and climb on the counter to peer out of the window. The two of them are standing there side by side, quiet now, their four eyes looking straight at me. The drake lowers his head to peck at something and I see that I have left a trail behind me, a scattering of red, yellow, blue and green plastic clothes-pegs like a child's toys left out on the grass at night.

I pull back in. The kitchen is full of flies. I take down the swatter from its nail on the wall and flick at them half-heartedly. Some of them die. One of them dies noisily on its back, buzzing and spinning round and round, its little legs moving in a dark blur. Others escape. And more still must sneak in all the time, at the edges of the door and the windows, constant reinforcements from the lazily swishing cows outside. I hang the fly-swatter up on the wall again and go to wash my hands. As the water trickles over and through my fingers I hear a cry from upstairs. She's awake. Sweat is running down inside my shirt. I shrug the damp fabric away from the small of my back. It's too hot. I almost trip over the open boxes as I run upstairs to lift her out of the cot. It's too hot to pack today. There is still time for all that. Tomorrow. Or the day after. I pick her up and dress her in fresh clothes and carry her outside, grabbing a few things from the kitchen as I pass through. When I reach into the car to strap her in her car-seat the metal buckle is already hot enough to burn my hand. I yelp and she looks at me. It's too hot even to cry. Her arms and legs hang out over the edges of the seat, limp as a doll's. I open all the windows and turn the key in the ignition. 'It's no good, Hannah,' I tell her. 'We can't stay in this place.'

We drive, up through Bayeux and then northwest towards the coast, to the beach you and I first visited together, just before you left. In spite of the weather, it isn't crowded – still more a place of pilgrimage than somewhere to sunbathe. I set Hannah free and she runs away from me across the wet sand, a small figure in a pink sunsuit, the fine hair caught in sun like a halo, her short arms flapping. A few gulls lift and fly away ahead of her, shrieking. The tide is out, withdrawing for what seems like miles, long tongues of salt water reaching down to the line of dark weed and broken shells where the waves break with a distant hiss. 'Hannah. Come here.' I run a few steps to catch up with her and turn her upside down in the air. She screams with surprise and delight. Then I clutch her to my hip and begin the long hot climb.

At the top of the cliffs there is that monument, do you remember? That ugly thing made of great blocks of stone, like a grim totem or a visitor from an alien planet. And the inscription in two languages. 'The allied forces landing on this

5

shore . . .' And above it, in the same stark upper-case lettering, '*Les forces alliées débarquent sur cette plage . . .*' We read them aloud to each other that day, the wind whipping the sand in our faces. And talked about your young uncle, one of the ones who didn't make it. And laughed. Because we were happy or irreverent enough that day to laugh at anything. Or did I imagine the laughter?

Now it seems inconceivable that we could have smiled, even. Over to my right the semicircular garden waits, with its 1557 names of the missing, your uncle's among them, the paths radiating from the centre like wheel-spokes or the rays of a child's sun. And beyond, the rows and rows of head-stones. 'Your great-uncle, Hannah,' I say to her. 'Look.' But she is happy, the sea-breeze ruffling her hair, ruffling mine, taking the metallic edge from the heat, turning this landscape of death into a landscape of sea-creatures. I hold her close and she looks up at me. I bend my face down to hers and we rub noses. She laughs, a wisp of her hair blowing across her face, catching at my mouth. It is all ancient history to her, as ir-relevant as Bunker Hill or Waterloo. She struggles against me to run free again. Everything is different now.

When we get back, Dominique is outside in front of the cottage, trudging backwards and forwards across the circle of gravel with cardboard boxes. Something clinks inside them as she loads them one by one into the back of the car. 'Hi,' she says. 'Just going to the dump. Have you got anything you want me to take?'

'It's all right. I've got so much stuff I'll have to go myself. A whole carful, probably.'

She pushes in the last load and comes towards me, wiping her weathered hands on the sides of her shorts. Her legs are like an old man's, spare and veiny. 'Sure?'

'I haven't sorted things out properly. I haven't really even started to pack.'

She screws up her eyes to look at me. 'When're you off?'

'I don't know. Not for a day or two.' I put Hannah down on the gravel at my feet and she sinks to her knees, raking her hands in it. One hand goes to her mouth. I pick her up again. 'Why? Do you need the cottage now? Have you got someone coming in?'

'Oh, no. It's yours. You've paid for it until the end of the month. You may as well make the most of it. I just wondered, that's all.'

'Not for a few days yet,' I say. 'I'll let you know.'

'Sure. And we can have a drink before you go.'

'All right.' It sounds ungracious.

She looks at me again. 'Well, you've been a very quiet tenant, I must say. No music, no parties, no drunken arguments or car doors slamming in the middle of the night. Not like Henry and Cara. And their baby. What was his name?'

'Josh.'

'Robert and I were saying how quiet you were. We barely even know you're there.' She laughs.

'Soon I won't be there.' Hannah is getting heavier on my hip. I turn and start to walk towards the cottage.

'Oh . . . One last thing.'

'What?' I say it almost rudely.

'Did the ducks bother you?'

'The ducks?'

'Were they after you this morning?'

'What makes you say that?' I am at the cottage door now. I fumble my key into the lock.

'Oh, nothing. I was a bit late feeding them, that's all. I just wondered.'

I turn my back on her. The door swings open on a buzz of waking flies.

I need to make one last visit to the Faculté. I'm not sure why, exactly. To tie up loose ends, any loose ends that might need tying. To say goodbye to the place, ugly and impersonal as it is. Folding one's clothes neatly on the chair before getting into bed to die. Something like that. I know there is nothing there for me, nothing I really have to see to. And anyway I have Hannah now. But I leave her with Dominique for the afternoon and set out.

It is August. The campus will be deserted. No one to see me come. No one to see me leave. Yet I park in a side-street and walk the last two blocks. The concrete buildings rise up in front of me.

The entrance foyer is almost empty. One or two foreign

students stand looking at notice-boards. Even the front steps have been swept of their usual litter of cigarette butts. The stairway echoes round me as I climb from the amphitheatres to the first floor.

I pass the doors of the locked classrooms. 101, where I met that first rowdy group of second-year scientists. 106, where that shy North African girl burst into tears, the time I gave her a 6 out of 20 for prose. 107, where the *maîtrise* lot sat with arms folded on a Friday afternoon, Marthe at the back, leaning sideways in her chair, the pockets of her shapeless cardigan heavy with nameless objects, her face turned to the window.

I reach the English staffroom. There is no one there, as I expected. And it is tidy, the usual mess of books and briefcases cleared or claimed for the summer. Only, on a side-table under the far window, stacks of photocopies. They are mine. I close my eyes for a moment and I can see them – passages from Stoppard, Hemingway, D. H. Lawrence. 'But no, he would not give in. Turning sharply, he walked towards the city's gold phosphorescence. His fists were shut, his mouth set fast. He would not take that direction, to the darkness . . .' I walk over to them and lift a corner of the top page. 'His fists were shut, his mouth set fast. He would not take that direction, to the darkness . . .' And another. '. . . to the darkness . . .' They are an embarrassment now, so much wasted literature for students who voted with their feet. I pick up the piles of paper one by one. I fill the two bags I have brought with me. I fill an empty file and clutch it to my chest with the other hand. I put it down again to balance a last sheaf as best I can. There are so many of them. So many words in the world, all of them in languages foreign to someone. I think of Hannah's few first words – *Mama, ink, pipi* – and manage to smile. Not so long ago we came into this world, inarticulate, groping to make ourselves understood, and now already we are leaving it.

But as I struggle to close the door behind me I hear footsteps. Lervain comes round the corner of the corridor, his greying head bent, humming something that could be Vivaldi. The top sheaf of papers slides from my awkward grip and spreads itself over the floor at my feet.

'Sorry, I . . .' Already I am kneeling to gather the loose pages. I can feel my face going red, the heat rising to my neck and outwards from the roots of my hair.

'May I help you?'

'No. No. It's all right. I'm sorry.' I stack the piles neatly again and stand up, brushing the dirt from my fingers to shake his outstretched hand.

He looks at me, his eyes crinkling. I have forgotten how disconcertingly young his face is. 'Are you leaving?'

'Soon.'

'May I help you with . . . these?'

'No. No.' He looks somehow unlike himself, dressed in a Lacoste shirt and casual trousers. 'Thank you.'

He peers down at me. Everything in his face expresses concern. Affection, almost. 'I'm so sorry.'

'Sorry?' It sounds half-witted, when I repeat it. 'For what?'

'Oh . . .' He shrugs. 'You know. That it didn't work out. You were the best, the most conscientious . . .' He leaves the sentence unfinished. 'I had hoped . . .'

'Yes,' I say. 'I hoped as well. Too bad. That's life.'

'Well. So you're going.'

'It looks like it.'

'Well. *Have a good journey. Have a good life.*' He says it in English. I've hardly ever heard him speak English, not since that first formal speech of welcome.

'*Je vous remercie, Monsieur,*' I say. I pick up the bags, the file, the papers.

Then he bends down and kisses me on both cheeks.

On the way home I decide to go to the supermarket. Not that I really need anything for myself, the time I have left is so short. But Hannah needs disposable nappies, and I've run out of *petits suisses* for her, and apple juice, and bananas. I stack the papers on the back seat and drive to Mammouth on the outskirts of town.

The car-park is half empty. It's too hot, even for the natives. I leave my little orange car as near as I can to the door and go in.

I am standing among the fruit and vegetables, a bunch of bananas in my hand, when a voice says, over my shoulder, 'Those are too green.' I jump and turn round. It is Marthe.

'They're all green.'

9

'You shouldn't buy fruit and vegetables in here, they're disgusting. You can find much better stuff at the market.'

'I haven't got time to go to the market.'

She purses her mouth slightly. She's wearing a T-shirt with a picture of Popeye and Olive Oyl on the front. Olive Oyl's face is a greenish colour. 'Say NO to spinach,' it says, in English. 'Don't be absurd. Markets are the real thing. Whereas this . . .' She gestures at a shelf stacked with tins of pet food.

'I haven't got time,' I say again. 'And it's too hot.'

She leans across me, reaching into the pile of fruit, lifting them and turning them over, inspecting the greenish hands one by one. Near the back she finds a bunch that is obviously riper than the rest, the skins uniformly speckled, without a bruise. 'Here. Try these.'

'Thanks.' I look down at what she has in her own basket. Biscottes, margarine, a starred bottle of cheap wine. 'You can get better wine, too, at your corner shop,' I tell her.

She grins then. 'I haven't seen you.'

'I haven't been around much. And I thought you were in the south.'

'I just got back.'

'How was it?'

'Okay. Well . . .' She shrugs. 'Not okay really. Folkloric. My family. French families.' She makes a face. For a moment I have the bizarre impression that she is going to spit.

'Listen . . .' I say.

'I'm listening.'

'Look . . . Have you just about finished?'

She glances down at her basket. 'Yes. Completely. I was just going towards the check-out, and then I saw you.'

'Let's go and have a drink.'

'If you want.' She's turned her back already, walking away from me towards the end of the aisle. 'Why not?'

We are sitting at the Etoile du Nord, outside, at a table on the pavement. She takes a long drink from her *sérieux*, pushes her short hair from her forehead and rubs her eyes with the heels of her hands. Then she leans back in her chair. She is taking it all in, the other tables, the shuttered grey façades, the striped awning of the florist's opposite. Then she leans forward across the table and speaks in a half-whisper. 'They're English.'

'Who?'

'That family at the corner table. Don't let them see you looking.'

'So what?' I say. The city is full of my compatriots at this time of year. There must be almost as many English people here as there are French. Though I've never been here before in August. But in spite of myself I turn slightly in my seat to look at them. A pleasant, boring-looking woman, in her forties, probably. A good-looking man with a moustache, who might be younger. Two teenage daughters, one dark, one blond. 'What about them?'

'Don't they look sweet?'

'Shut up. They'll hear you.'

'They won't know what we're saying.'

'I wouldn't bet on it.'

'The husband might. I shouldn't think she would. She looks too . . .'

'She looks like me.'

Marthe raises an eyebrow.

'She looks like me, in twenty years.'

She doesn't seem to hear me. She says suddenly, 'Are you coming out to Francis's?'

'When?'

'Tomorrow. For the weekend.'

I frown. 'Can anyone go?'

'I think so. There aren't many people around at the moment.'

'Who else is going?'

'Laurence. Paul and Mireille. They're the only ones I know about.'

'And you,' I say. 'I'll think about it.'

'Sarah . . .' Marthe puts her elbows on the table and rests her chin on her hand. She narrows her eyes. 'Sarah, I didn't tell you. I'm glad you're leaving,' she says.

'I guessed.'

'Really very glad.'

I look at her to see if she is smiling. I hesitate. I pitch the words carefully. 'Any particular reason?'

'*Because you're a terrible teacher,*' she says, in English.

'Terrible, or *terrible*?'

'Terrible.'

'Thanks.' I put some change on the dish and stand up to go. Behind me I hear one of the daughters saying, 'I'm all right! Leave me alone!' I can tell from her voice that she is close to tears.

As I drive home the stored heat of the road comes up to meet me in a rising shimmer. I leave the suburbs behind, the villages, one after the other, in a grey blur. In one of them a dusty bus is disgorging its passengers. I overtake it and drive on.

And then at last the cool of a forest. Through the open windows I can smell the shadow. Pine-needles, the green of moss, small plants growing at the verges. I turn in along a rutted dirt road and switch off the engine. I get out and lock the car behind me. I walk through the damp shade for perhaps half a mile, the hairs on my arms lifting in the slight breeze that moves under the branches. I even shiver. I sit down on a fallen trunk and look up. Above me the treetops almost meet, a long straight road into nothing. Next to my hand, the layered frills of an unnameable brown fungus. I reach out to break a piece off but it resists me, tough as rubber. *Terrible*. Terrible. I take a deep breath. It is like opening my mouth to freshly turned earth. I close my eyes.

Francis lives in Mériniers, a long way out, perhaps twenty miles south of the city. I've only been there about twice. A brief visit in April. And that first time, when we were first together, with Cara and Henry. I'm not sure I even know the way.

At one point I stop in a small village to ask. *'Mériniers, oui, il faut prendre à gauche, là-bas, juste avant le tournant. Là où vous voyez la petite maison grise . . .'* I thank him and drive on. Fermenonville, the sign says, as I leave the last scattered buildings behind, the name struck through with a red line.

But when I get there, there is no mistaking it. I can see it all again through the sharp clear sun of that autumn, trapped in glass. A fold in the hills, and we come down among pointed roofs, a small church with a steeple like a grey needle. Trees that were brown and orange then, that are heavy and green now. Hannah squeals with delight as we coast down the steep hill. I can't look round at her, but I know she is pointing, her whole hand stuck out in that way babies have when they want something, her plump forefinger extended in the direction of the world. We drive down into the little triangular square, and I follow my nose. Sharp left, second right. Right again. The narrow houses are built almost on top of one another. I draw up at the kerb and kneel in my seat to undo Hannah's buckle and lift her out. 'We're here,' I tell her. 'We've arrived.' She tries to wriggle away from me to run on the pavement but I hold on tightly, and she starts to wail. I don't let go.

The façade of Francis's house is unprepossessing, a grey cottage like any of the others, flush with the pavement. Built on to it on one side, an odd structure of what looks like corrugated iron held together with wooden struts. The paint is flaking, the wood of some of the posts rotting near the base. I kick one of them and my foot makes a shower of soft splinters. And on the other side, another cottage, almost identical to the first.

Francis himself opens the door, his hair brushed forwards across his forehead as usual, shining in the light from the street. A pale blue lawn shirt that must have cost 700 francs. Immaculate light trousers. 'Sarah,' he says. He looks past Hannah at my dusty little Dyane, parked in the road. I see that someone has written '*A besoin d'être lavé*' with a wet finger on the nearside wing.

'Am I the first?'

'Come in.' He stands aside and gestures towards the interior. I lift Hannah and carry her in my arms up a short flight of stone steps and into a dark passage. Then up more steps and into a room.

It's a strange room, not like any room I have ever been in, before or since. A heavy dark oak table, dark chairs, mahogany side-tables. A lamp with a china base in the shape of a nymph. A metal standard lamp that is all twining vines and burnished petals. A low coffee-table with expensive-looking books of reproductions. On the walls, framed facsimiles of some kind of writing, some of it in French, some in English. A perfect écritoire that might have belonged to Madame de Sévigné.

And on the other side, the open door. It leads down more steps into a conservatory – the street side of it rotting wood

13

and rusting iron, true, but the roof and garden side open to the light. I look up and see branches, distorted slightly by a flaw in the glass. And beyond it the other cottage on the other side, where I know Francis has his bedroom, a mirror image of this first house, its grey twin. Hannah escapes from my arms and totters down the steps into the conservatory with a squeal, her feet clattering on the old tiles. She has seen the bar football machine. But she is too small. If she stretches up she can just touch the handles. Behind me I hear Francis laugh.

'Has anyone else come yet?'

'Oh . . . Marthe's coming later. She's working until six. Laurence is here.' He makes a vague gesture. 'Somewhere.'

'And Paul and Mireille?'

'They couldn't make it.' He smiles slightly. 'Sorry.'

It's hard to sustain any sort of conversation with him. He's too intelligent. 'Do you mind if I go out and have a wander round?'

But he is visibly relieved. 'Do. You might bump into Laurence. She's . . .' He brushes a speck from his trousers. 'And Marthe will be here soon after six.'

I let Hannah run away from me down the path, a small figure staggering into the distance. I stand watching her for a moment from the terrace. A few rusting chairs are grouped round a white-painted iron table, one of them knocked over on its side and left to lie. And the top of the table itself is strewn with drying walnuts. *Un noyer gaulé.* The phrase comes into my mind unbidden, without explanation. '*Gauler*, to beat (fruit-tree, walnut-tree).' That must have been the nut-tree, those twisted branches I caught sight of through the glass.

I walk down into the garden, following the same path Hannah took. A few straggly roses, uncared for. A vegetable patch enclosed by box hedges. Some of the crops are recognisable, but some are strange to me. Then the garden opens out into an orchard, the grass up round my ankles, and sheep grazing. I look at them. There is something vaguely odd about them. Some rare long-haired breed. They move slowly over the grass like large whitish slugs, casting shadows. I can hear them eating the grass, with a sound of tearing. Hannah runs up to me suddenly from nowhere and buries her face in my skirt.

'Where have you been, darling?' She lets go of my legs, but

14

still holds on tightly to one hand. 'What a lovely garden! It's full of secret places. You show me.'

She laughs up at me then and half-stumbles, the long grass up round her short legs. She is wading through green. She pulls on my hand and I follow, treading in the small craters of her footsteps. She pulls me over to where a circle of trees half conceals a dappled space.

A girl is sitting on the ground, the summer landscape falling away in front of her, her long light hair over her shoulders. Laurence. She is leaning back, her hands drowned in grass, sun rippling across her face, her eyes closed. About ten feet away from her my daughter stops, as if she doesn't dare go any closer. Side by side we stand watching. The beautiful girl. Her closed face. Then she opens her eyes, squints up at the sun, turns and sees us. She smiles and opens her arms to Hannah, but Hannah tugs at my hand, trying to run away. Laurence looks over her head, at me. 'Francis is so lucky,' she says.

I have put on different clothes for dinner. I have left Hannah asleep on the bed, already exhausted with the excitement and the heat. When I come into the room, Laurence and Francis are standing together against the light.

They turn towards me as I come in, and smile, the same kind of smile. Identical glasses in their hands. Marthe looks up from the window-seat. 'Can I get you something to drink?' Francis says.

'What're you drinking?'

'Martini.'

'Thank you. That would be very nice.'

He leaves the room and comes back a moment later with a tall glass in his hand. Its sides are sweating. He gives it to me and picks up his own. '*A la tienne.*'

'*A la vôtre.*' In her corner, Marthe makes a face. I take a long swig of the drink. It isn't as strong as I expected, only the faintest suspicion of gin. Hardly more than Martini and melting ice-cubes. 'When did you get here?' I ask her.

'About half an hour ago.'

The ice clinks against the wall of the glass. 'Did you find it easily?'

'Of course.'

'You only have to ask someone. They'll all tell you. *Le monsieur cultivé, celui qui a les moutons.*' Laurence laughs, but there is no irony. She is looking up at him sideways under her hair. She shakes it back from her face, moving closer to him. He steps forward to the table and picks up a handful of peanuts from a delicate cut-glass bowl.

'Tell us about your research, Francis.' Laurence blots her mouth on a napkin and takes a mouthful of wine.

'Oh . . .' He picks up a knife at the side of his plate and turns it so that the light from the candles flickers in the blade. 'You don't really want to hear about all that.'

'Lervain was telling me a little about it the other day. It sounded fascinating.'

There is a silence. I can hear my mouth chewing.

Then Marthe's voice, low and serious. 'I'd like to hear about it. But not if you really don't want to tell us.'

Francis relaxes visibly. He looks directly at her. 'It's the grail motif,' he says. 'But in twentieth-century literature. Jack London, Hemingway, Styron, Updike . . .'

The fork is halfway to my mouth. It stays there, suspended. 'You surprise me,' I say.

He laughs easily. 'Why?'

'I'd always put you down as a seventeenth-century man. I've known you all these months and I always assumed that that's what you were.'

'I do fill in for colleagues sometimes. It's good for the soul.'

'For whose soul?'

'For the soul of the student body,' he says, and laughs again.

Laurence is looking at him with undisguised admiration. 'Don't be modest,' she says. 'They couldn't manage without you. Lervain told me.'

'Oh, if Lervain told you . . .' It is my own voice.

No one says anything. The silence is beginning to be uncomfortable. Then Francis coughs. 'Seriously, though, Sarah . . .' He is offering me more wine. I cover my glass with my hand. 'You shouldn't be dismissive of him. I hear what they're all saying. But he's no fool.' He flashes a brief look at Laurence, but she is absorbed in the food on her plate. 'And he's more influential than you might think.'

16

'I thought all that was impossible here,' I say. 'I thought Heads of Department were democratically elected.'

'They are.'

'And strictly temporary.'

No one answers. I turn to look at Francis. He is smiling at me from under the hair, an odd, constrained smile. 'Even so . . .' he says gently.

My face feels suddenly like cardboard. 'It's all right. I know exactly how influential he is. I just don't care any more, that's all.' I crumple my napkin beside my plate and push my chair back. 'If you'll all excuse me I'll just go and check on Hannah,' I say.

When I come down again they are already on the dessert, some special creation. Laurence has two helpings. 'Francis, did you really make this?' Her eyes are luminous, flickering with the candle-flames. For a moment we eat in silence, as the chocolate melts on our tongues.

And then something seems to happen. I glance at my watch.

'You travel through white countries, snowy wastes of paper,' Francis is saying, 'fishing in rivers, wherever the road takes you . . .' And Laurence is nodding her fair head. The candles blowing in the draught from the open window, the flames flickering almost horizontal, a puff of dark smoke rising towards the ceiling, licking at the expensive furniture, the immaculate plaster, losing itself in the noises of the summer evening, voices, the crack of dry walnut-shells, strange sheep tearing at the grass. Somewhere, an owl. A dream of voices from home, Hannah, another country. My future tipping towards me like a dark cup. I look at my watch again. The hands haven't moved. I notice that I am still sitting on my chair, my elbows on the table, my chin on my hands, my napkin neatly folded beside my plate. Laurence to my right, and Francis still opposite, smiling into his glass. The wooden legs still supporting us all.

Francis stands up. He has left us. Then he is back, with something in his arms. He sits down on the window-seat, cradling the thing in his lap. It appears to be a lute. He plucks at the strings, a teasing sequence of discrete notes, nothing resembling a tune. '. . . made for me by a man in Bayeux,' he is saying. 'A real craftsman.' And then, 'Let me show you. It's a question of modes.'

Laurence is at his elbow, leaning over him, over the instrument, the ends of her long hair brushing the strings.

'Diatonic arrangements within the octave.' He begins to hum softly. The humming and the plucked accompaniment seem to come from two different places.

'Almost like modes of speech . . . or modes of engagement.' Laurence's voice is low, intimate. We are not supposed to hear. 'Or modes of narration.'

'*Tripes à la mode*,' Marthe says to me, under her breath.

And I want to laugh. Not just ordinary laughter, but a huge, unstoppable mirth that gathers in a hard lump under my ribs and begs to be let out. Laughing to save my life. 'Excuse me,' I say, to the room in general. 'I must just . . .'

I slip out into the passage, not stopping to put on the light, making for the toilet. But before I can reach it, the wave engulfs me, rising from somewhere in my stomach, almost choking me with the effort of keeping it back. I let it come. I sink down in the dark, my back against the wall, laughing noiselessly, my eyes streaming. A pool of water collects next to my nose, sharp and salty as grief. I turn my head slightly and it rolls down my cheek, losing itself somewhere in my clothes. My whole body is shaking.

And Marthe is there beside me, laughing as helplessly as I am. I feel her presence in the darkness. She's gasping, brushing her sleeve across her face. 'It was the cake.' Something hits me on the shoulder. Her hand? 'He put something in the cake.' She leans forward, holding her knees and burying her face in them, not touching me now. Her laughter still reaches me through the knot of her arms, muffled, as if from a long way off. I hear her gulp for breath. 'And Laurence had two helpings.'

When I wake in the morning they are already at breakfast. For a moment I lie there listening, waiting for the dream to recede. Shreds of past conversation and faces, my own inept remarks, a sudden burst of French, unexpectedly fluent. The past. The future. Downstairs, the chink of a spoon on the side of a bowl, the rasp of a knife along a crust. Hannah stirs at my elbow and I watch her wake. She sticks her small bottom in the air,

18

under the tent of sheet. Then she rolls over and starts to suck her thumb, her eyes still shut. I brush the wisp of sandy hair gently back from her face and she opens her eyes.

They look up when we enter the room. I sit Hannah on a chair, on a pile of cushions, so that she can just see over the table. She reaches for the jam and I rescue it, placing it carefully on the other side, just out of range. I spoon the chocolate powder into her bowl and start to peel her a banana. 'Did you sleep well?' someone asks me.

I glance up. It is Laurence who has spoken. There's no sign of anything unusual. She is cool, dressed in a cream-coloured shirt that looks freshly ironed. 'Very well,' I say. 'Thanks. And you?'

I am just quick enough to catch something – I'm not sure what – the slightest movement of her body in his direction, irrepressible as breathing. 'Yes,' she says. She dips the buttered bread in her coffee and leaves it there for a moment, seeming to forget to raise it to her mouth. She half-smiles, watching the butter melt into little beads of fat that spread and meet on the surface like a thin crust of ice.

'Where's Marthe?'

Francis stands up to fetch the fresh coffee, the boiled milk. 'I've no idea. Still asleep, I suppose. Did you want her for something?'

I'm tired. I blink, but my eyes still feel heavy, the morning sunlight slightly blurred across the table. I don't know how to talk to them, which language to use. 'I was wondering . . .' I can feel the flush rising to my neck. 'I thought she might need a lift back.'

'I don't think so. She came under her own steam, didn't she, Laurence? Her car's out on the street.'

'You can ask her,' Laurence says, looking past me, through the window. I turn and see Marthe coming towards us from somewhere at the back of the house, the orchard, possibly. I hear the metal catch of the door as she opens it. I hear the door swing to behind her.

But she doesn't come in, to where we are. I hear something slam, and then the dull low sound of something rolling. Then a sharp crack.

Francis's eyes twinkle with amusement. 'She's beaten us to it,' he says. 'The early worm.'

We stand up one by one and go out into the conservatory. I help Hannah from her throne of cushions and she goes down the stone steps sideways, just ahead of me. Marthe is standing at the bar football table. Her hand reaches from one handle to the other and gives a desultory flick. There is a crash, and the sound of the ball dropping, somewhere inside the machine.

'Shall we show them? What do you think?' Francis is looking at me, turning back his immaculate cuffs.

For a while the white ball shoots backwards and forwards, coming to an awkward stop every time one of my men touches it, jumping out of the frame once when Laurence spins the handle, chipping an old tile at one corner. She is unexpectedly good.

But Francis is brilliant. Inept as I am, we end up winning. After a while I take to standing back whenever I see the ball coming in my direction, willing him to take the handles out of my hands. And Laurence is losing her self-composure, the long hair flying as she spins the poles. She is shouting now, each time she scores a goal, her cheeks flushed, her delicate wrists quick as his. Marthe plays placidly on, refusing to be fazed. Finally we are victorious. Laurence straightens her back and glares at Francis over the ranked chipped heads of the painted men.

I leave Hannah with them and walk out into the garden. The rows of vegetables look somehow more ambivalent now, the strange sheep more normal. I think I hear someone call my name, but when I turn round there is no one. The long shadows almost cover the grass, the dew still on it from the cooler air of the small hours, individual blades sparkling. And when I come up the path again, Francis and Laurence are moving backwards and forwards at the windows in what looks like a kind of dance, clearing the breakfast things. Francis glances up, the butter-dish in one hand, a clean knife in the other. 'Marthe's gone,' he says. 'She had to leave. She told me to say goodbye.' He looks suddenly tired and hung-over. His lute is still on the window-seat, only slightly less ludicrous in this light than it was before.

The morning passes. Hannah runs backwards and forwards under the trees in the orchard, a small vertical figure among the horizontal backs of the sheep. In the end she flops down beside me on the grass. Her eyes go wide, the pupils dilated. Her thumb moves towards her mouth.

To sleep. I close my own eyes, and it is like swimming in my own darkness, the patterns of blood-vessels on my retina a web of red. Voices. The continuo of dialogue with the people who might save me. The people who speak to me always without even knowing they are speaking, in their own tongue or in mine. Laurence, her French voice slightly distorted by distaste. The bland kindly voice of Lervain. I shiver suddenly, incongruously. You. In the red tangle of threads I see Hannah's small body forming, an inverted red fish, a flicker of blood caught in the light.

When I go back in, Francis looks at me enquiringly, raising an eyebrow. 'Lunch?'

I can't believe it is lunchtime already. My watch must be playing tricks.

I help him carry the plates and cutlery out on to the terrace. He sweeps the walnuts aside into an old rush basket someone has left lying on its side on the ground. Then we sit there, the four of us, and eat, in silence.

After the meal, Francis stands up. It looks almost like a signal for someone to leave. But he says, 'One last game?'

'I'm sorry?'

'A last game of babyfoot, before you go?'

'But there are only three of us.'

'You and Laurence can be a team. I'll play on my own. That's what we did when Hoad Ashley came.'

'Hoad Ashley? The narratology man? He came here?'

'A few months ago.'

'And you got him to play bar football?'

'Why not? It's a legitimate branch of human endeavour.'

'And did he deconstruct the game, as soon as it was over?'

'No. He was talking to Laurence.' Francis looks at her sideways, teasing. 'He obviously found something about the conversation fairly absorbing. I couldn't tell you what it was.'

I look over at Laurence. Her expression is disdainful, but she says nothing.

'Well?' It is Francis. 'Are you both ready for this?'

'I suppose I am,' I say.

We troop down the steps into the conservatory again. We take up our positions at the handles. But when Francis leans down to pull the lever nothing happens. There is only the sound of the spring, without the usual grumble from inside the machine. Laurence looks up at him in surprise.

But he is no wiser than she is. I reach down and waggle my fingers in the slot but it is quite empty. Then I see Hannah standing in a corner.

I go over to her and kneel on the broken tiles at her feet. 'Where are the balls, Hannah?' I ask her. 'What did you do with them?'

She looks at me steadily. Then she shakes her head.

'Where did you put them, sweetheart? We want to play.'

Francis is at my shoulder, bending over us in concern. 'Could she have swallowed them? Would she have put them in her mouth, do you think?'

I pretend to look stern. 'Did you put them in your mouth, darling? Are they all in your tummy now?' I put out my hand and pat her little round stomach through the light cotton dungarees.

She turns her head away, giggling.

'Where are they?' I say more firmly. I reach out and grab her by the shoulders but she wriggles away from me and runs through the open door into the garden, flapping her arms. She falls on to the old basket, hugging it to her chest. I prise her from it gently and tip it up. The white balls fall out of it like round eggs, in a rain of nuts.

And now it is time to say goodbye. The car is packed, all Hannah's stuff stacked in the boot in a colourful pile of toys and miscellaneous equipment. In one of the front pockets, a package of disposable nappies bulges its plastic-covered sides, its printed picture of an ideal baby smiling his frozen smile. Dark-haired. French. Nothing at all like Hannah. She is complaining now, over-tired and grumpy. I turn my face away from her as I strap her into her seat and fasten the buckle.

I get out of the car one last time. Francis and Laurence are standing together in the open doorway. Francis moves out on to the pavement to see me go, outlined against the unlikely flaking structure of the conservatory. He bends to kiss me. Laurence stretches out her hand. 'Well, goodbye.'

Francis looks suddenly embarrassed. 'I suppose we may not see one another again.'

The pavement under my feet is irregular, the stones of the narrow kerb pushed out of alignment by heat or frost. 'I suppose not.'

'Well . . . perhaps one of these days, in London or somewhere.'

'Yes. Possibly.'

Laurence raises her head. 'You should say goodbye to Lervain.'

'I have. I went into the *Fac* the other day and bumped into him.'

Uncharacteristically she is biting her lip. 'He didn't want to lose you. He told me.'

Behind me I can hear Hannah, her wails of protest getting steadily louder. 'I'm not lost.'

'And you should call in and meet Helen, before you leave.'

'I don't know Helen.'

'She's very agreeable.'

'Christ!' I say. '*Agreeable?* What's that supposed to mean?'

Francis steps forward suddenly and gives me a hug. It is completely unexpected. 'She's about as agreeable as you were, when you first came. And probably a better loser too.'

'We didn't lose,' I say. 'Not this time.'

For a moment he still holds me tightly. 'Take care of yourself.'

'And you.' I glance at Laurence, over the fabric of his sleeve. 'Both of you. I'll send you my address, as soon as I have one.

And then I am driving away. The narrow grey streets open to swallow us, Hannah suddenly quiet and sleepy behind me. I look back as I turn the corner. They are standing close together now. Laurence seems to be smiling. There is something pale on her shoulder, a small, limp animal. I realise it must be his hand.

Marthe's flat is in a newish concrete block on the edge of town. I know which are her windows. I look up at them and see that the shutters are closed.

I sit in the car then and wait, Hannah still asleep behind me. The sound of pigeons drifts in through the open car windows with the cooler air of evening. Someone drives into the car-park and parks. A man in a suit walks past me, jingling a bunch of keys. Above me, in a flat diagonally below Marthe's, a light goes on.

Her windows are still dark. In the end I scribble a few words on a scrap of paper and go in, leaving Hannah slumped in her seat. I go up to the fourth floor and ring the bell. No answer. A sudden loud blast from a television as someone just beneath me opens and closes a door. I get down on my knees to push the note into the crack. Then I think better of it. As I half-run down the stairs I am already tearing it into fragments. White butterflies. Just at the bottom of the stairwell there is a row of small dustbins, lined up against the wall. I lift the lid of the nearest and poke the little torn pieces of paper well down inside.

The flat where Helen lives is the flat we used to live in, rue Daumier, on the ground floor, the high metal shutters giving straight out on to the street. Sometimes if we got up late someone would lean a bike against them, and when we folded them back we would hear the crash of falling metal. And every morning that loud procession of two-wheeled and four-wheeled vehicles, taking over the city, like a swarm of grotesquely magnified insects.

I ring the bell and wait for the buzzer before pushing the familiar door open. The first time Hannah struggles and takes my mind off what I'm doing and the door stays shut. But the second time I catch it as it buzzes. Helen is standing at the open inner door, Chryssa half-hiding behind her. 'I'm glad you could come,' she says. 'Hello, darling. Aren't you lovely?' She reaches out and strokes Hannah's hair back from her forehead as naturally as if my daughter were her own child. Hannah looks up at her and smiles.

'Well,' I say.

'We haven't really met.'

'Only that once.'

'We didn't get a chance to talk to each other.'

'No.'

'And I didn't even remember you had a little girl.'

Hannah struggles against me. I put her down and she staggers off across the lino. Chryssa runs after her and grabs her hand. I laugh. 'She's my best-kept secret,' I say.

I sit down on one of the steel and formica chairs. Helen pulls out the chair opposite and leans to lift the lid of a teapot on the table. 'I'm sorry. It's a bit stewed.'

'Don't worry.'

'No. I'll make some more.' She gets up and starts to boil water in a dented saucepan. 'It's proper tea. I brought it with me from England.'

'Lovely.'

She looks embarrassed. 'Of course, you'll be back there in a few days. And I'm only just arriving.' She frowns, shifting from one foot to the other as she waits for the water to boil. 'But I'm so glad to have had the chance to meet you before you left. *Both* of you.' She bites her lip. 'I mean . . .'

'I know. It's all right. They told you. It doesn't take long with the old grapevine.'

'They said that you and someone called Joseph . . .' She hesitates, and looks down. The water is boiling furiously but she doesn't seem to notice.

'We lived here. You know that.'

'Here. In town.'

'Here in this flat.'

'Oh.' She's taken aback. 'They didn't . . .'

'It's okay. It doesn't matter. I got this offer of a cottage out near Chanville, that someone else moved out of. That's the way it is. And it's much nicer, really, for Hannah, there's a garden with a pond, and ducks and things . . .' I hear my voice trail off. 'And with a car . . . And anyway, I'm leaving.'

'When?'

'In a couple of days. I'm not sure. It depends how long it takes me to pack up.'

'Not that easy with . . .' She turns and looks over to where the two small girls are crouching side by side over a pile of wooden animal figures. 'Don't let her put that in her mouth, Chryssa. She's only little, remember.' Then, to me, 'Do you need any help?' She is making the tea at last, the steam rising out of the mouth of the pot as she pours in the water. I miss the usual strings, dangling from the side like price-tags.

'I don't think so.' I raise my eyebrows. 'Do you?'

'With settling in?' she says. 'Oh, no. But thanks. I'm a bit worried about Chryssa and school, that's the only thing. There's quite a lot of paperwork. But the *maternelle*'s just round the corner. And I suppose it'll be all right.'

'Why shouldn't it be all right?'

'Oh . . . You know. The language barrier, and all that. All these little French kids with satchels on their backs and classy shoes.'

'You can get Chryssa a satchel.'

'Yes. Yes, of course I can. I'm just worried she won't talk to anyone, that's all. Or they won't talk to her. That it'll make her withdrawn or something. And it'll be my fault, for wanting to come.'

'She'll be fine,' I say. 'Stop worrying. Kids always are. They're amazingly adaptable. It's the rest of us that need worrying about.'

'Yes,' she says, and smiles. A rare smile. I wonder if I can see tears in her eyes. 'You're right. Of course. And look at you, you've been through it all already, having a baby here, and everything.'

'Everything.'

She lifts the pot and starts to pour the tea at last, a brown stream far stronger than either of us would ever dream of drinking in England. She lifts the glass bowl to her lips. 'What *is* the French for "satchel"?' she asks me.

If you were here, you would say I was procrastinating. When you left, it was all so easy. One night you were still here, in my bed. And the next you were in Paris. And the night after that you were back in Boston, among friends.

Slowly I begin seriously to pack. I haul out the metal trunk from its corner under the eaves and drag it on to the landing. The lid opens with a creak. A flake of rust falls from one of the hinges. Nothing inside but some old wrapping-paper and a short piece of string.

The books, first of all. My big Harraps, the Petit Larousse, still smelling faintly of floodwater, its pages stained and curling at the edges, the illustration of the ogive arch tinted

26

sepia like an old photograph, the picture of Camus still even younger than he was when he died.

The tapes. The notes, one copy of every sheet I have put together over these past months, just in case I might need any of them again. All the work I did, the days I spent in the section library gleaning suitable material, the nights I sat scratching my head for something to give purpose and direction to the endless oral sessions with students who hardly ever showed up, let alone spoke. The books I combed for examples of English humour, *le fameux humour anglais,* anything to make them laugh. The heavy-eyed mornings when you would tease me about it. Not letting me forget.

The shoes. Winter boots and trainers. The court shoes I wore to the departmental dinner. My winter coat, the thick jumpers, almost absurd in this heat. The jeans and skirts and blouses. The letters from home.

Bit by bit the cottage is being emptied of identity, reverting to its ordinary state. Soon it will be as it was when I first moved in, just the sofa and armchairs, the little table with the lamp, the brick shelves with their battered functional saucepans, the bed. The cot.

But in the drawer in the base of the wardrobe, under the big mirror, I find a whole bag stuffed full of unfamiliar junk. It must have been left by Henry and Cara. I've never opened this particular drawer until now.

I up-end the carrier-bag and tip everything out at my feet. Stacking plastic cups in garish primary colours. Board-books, their corners chewed and fraying. A baby's soft hairbrush. Folded Babygros, the nap worn transparent at the toes. I shake them out and hold them up in front of me at arm's length. But they are too small already for Hannah. 3–6 months. 0–3. Even the largest ones look shrunken, reduced by too much washing. She is well past all this now.

Then something catches my eye. A cassette, half under the lid of the trunk, in shadow. I pick it up and turn it over. *L'Enfance du Christ,* one of yours. *Oh, par pitié, secourez-nous. Laissez-nous reposer chez vous.* Perhaps I should post it back to you. It was a tape I always hated. Now you've gone, I don't have to listen.

It is still so hot. Even long after dark, the cottage seems to trap the heat inside its walls. When I have closed the lid I go outside into the garden and stand for a while looking out over the pond. No sound from the ducks. No owls, no sound from the cows. The world has gone quiet. Across the field beyond the far trees the sky flickers and jumps with light. Thunder rumbles in the distance. A sudden many-pronged fork of lightning, spectacular as something in a film.

I go upstairs to the bedroom. In here it's even hotter. My T-shirt is sticking to my back. But Hannah sleeps through it all. I lean over the cot and try to make out her face in the dim light from the landing.

She is breathing regularly, the sheet thrown off and her little body going up and down at a rhythm faster than my own, the rhythm of a child's sleep. I pull the sheet up over her gently. She doesn't wake.

I go over to the window and open it wider. No sound in the lane either, except distant laughter and voices through other open windows. The lights of the farmhouse glimmer at me from halfway up the hill. For a fraction of a second they are extinguished as the whole room behind me is lit in a white flash. Almost instantaneously I hear the thunderclap, right overhead. I turn to look over my shoulder at Hannah's dark shape in the cot, but she hasn't woken. And then the rain comes, a hiss, an army walking quietly on leaves. And the smell of wet grass rises, cooler, together with the smell of the earth.

The wind has come up suddenly, sweeping the rain towards me in black sheets across the field, hitting the stones of the cottage on this side. I realise I am drenched. I draw back in and close the window, the rain blowing against it and pouring down the glass. Battening down the hatches, securing every-thing against the typhoon. Alone at sea.

But there is Hannah. She sleeps through it all. The roof can't leak while she is under it. The trunk and boxes and cases I have will yawn open and I shall pile my things into them steadily layer by layer until they contain my life. Our life. And the weather can do what it likes, as irrelevant as Lervain, Marthe, Laurence. In Boston, for all I know, it could be snow-ing. No storm can touch me now I have a child.

2

I TRY TO REMEMBER that first moment, how she first appeared to me. I try to remember it for you, in case you should ever ask me, to fix it under a sheen of reflected light, so it can never get away.

It wasn't an easy birth. Not a particularly bad one either, if you can believe what they tell you. I shut my eyes and remember. The doctor. The nurse with the southern accent you could cut with a knife, almost incomprehensible, her *'Allez, doucemaing. Ne poussez pas encorr'* coming and going between the bad dreams. The way that young intern tried to draw me out on the subject of my research as he took hold of the forceps. *'Respirez. Ne poussez pas. Encore une.'* The key to the celebratory liqueur cabinet finally turning in the lock. And Hannah on my body like a warm fish. Her bruised head.

And between the nights of crying and pacing, the days of laundry and nursing and pacing, I catch it still, that first sight of her, her first raw cry, the smell of her on my skin. The joy of complete erasure. The past that is wiped out, totally, by her unwitting presence, the future that will never happen now. Our silly apology for a life ending at her cradle. The sheer fatigue of choosing usurped by this, purely physical, fatigue. Her small face that hardly resembles yours, that looks nothing at all like my own. She is so *sweet*, a wanted child. Would I ever really be able to explain to you just how sweet, just how wanted, she is?

Now you have gone, there are only the two of us. Hannah's small body is half-slumped on my knee like a bag of warm flour, my left hand on her back, just below the shoulders, rubbing. My right hand supports her chin. And in the big mirror of the *armoire*, her small twin, its dark head nodding drowsily in unison with hers. It is just getting light. 4.30 a.m. and the trees in the lane just beginning to come out of their darkness, the cows lurching to their knees, not yet starting to moo. Hannah's face is pointing towards the window, her eyes wide open. But unfocused: she can't see what's out there. Can she smell it, the night still on the grass, that smell of early summer? Can she hear all the same sounds I hear, the first wood-pigeons in the clump of trees by the barn, a cuckoo somewhere over the fields? Traffic, up on the main road. Would she recognise her name?

And you have never seen her. You will be in Maine already, standing on the deck of your parents' summer house, thinking it is time to go to bed. You're procrastinating, looking up at the stars. They are so bright, brighter than they can ever be here, where we are never far enough from the city. You can hear waves crashing on rocks, somewhere below the house. You can hear your sister's music, your parents' sleepy voices. You see and hear everything but us.

Soon I shall send you a photograph. I have a whole sheaf of them, the ones they took in the clinic the day she was born. She's wearing a wool bonnet, very chic, very French, to keep her head warm. If you were here I would show you. And you would look at the pictures with me and laugh.

I rub my hand round and round on her back and she belches. Her mouth hangs slightly open and a sour white ribbon of milk trickles from her chin. My fingers play across the little knobs of her sagging spine.

She begins to whimper slightly, writhing as if she were in pain, raking her closed fists across her face and turning her head from side to side, screwing up her eyes. Then her face goes red and her mouth opens wider. And she starts to cry, the first inhuman wail giving way to rhythmic rasps of sound that must be audible to anyone for miles around. As if on cue, my body starts to ache.

But she has been fed already. As she still gasps, I change her nappy, telling myself not to listen. She is purple now, her small features crumpled and ugly. I hoist her to my shoulder and pace the room with her, backwards and forwards in front of the window, until she is calmer. The floorboards creak under our combined weight.

And then abruptly the crying is over. The warm mass of her against my shoulder feels suddenly different in quality, more acquiescent, sleepier. Her fist is against my chin, the fingers uncurling slightly, damp. Very carefully I ease myself down on to the window-sill without waking her. The cows are mooing properly now. A voice calls softly in French. I hear the click of a gate. And there is sun now in the treetops, almost horizontal, shining right into my eyes, back-lighting each leaf.

It is only when she is asleep that I can really see us. That chaotic first meeting in the departmental staff room. 'Our very own Bostonian,' I remember Paul saying, when Lervain introduced you. 'He'll be teaching that new film course you may have heard about.' Just for a second, our eyes met. Then those first weeks, the whole lot of us laughing, talking in French, in English. Your lean face on the far side of the table, candlelit, saying something earnest to Laurence. Me listening, my mind drifting in and out of the sentences, watching you watch her. You hardly seemed to notice me there at all. Only that one glance – ironic? quizzical? – as you shrugged on your jacket to leave. And yet I was the one you sent that note to, the next morning. I was the one you moved in with.

Our little flat. The battered pans on the stove, the glass door of the oven that would never shut properly. The water gurgling in the bulbous cast iron radiators. The whine of the Mobylettes that would wake us every morning, when it was still dark. Your head on the pillow. It's only now, when I look at Hannah asleep on her mattress, that I begin to understand what it was you wanted.

Something you weren't able to find here with me, obviously. Something you're more likely to come across on the other side of the Atlantic, with new friends, or old ones. Perhaps you go and visit Henry and Cara? You play with Josh, even, down on your knees on the rug, among the plastic blocks and the animals. 'Doing your own thing,' as Cara used to call it. Your own thing, whatever that is, doesn't stop you from playing with their kid.

Are you with another woman now? Almost certainly, though Cara didn't tell me. And the woman is attractive, childless, her body slim and taut, as undamaged as yours. Her name is Jennifer, or Robin. She's not a teacher – or if she is, she's a good one, with no hesitations or inadequacies, no moments of sudden mental paralysis, no favourites. She has a hard-edged New York accent that makes you laugh. And you do your own thing with her. She has no child to stop you. I turn to look at Hannah asleep in a strip of moonlight, and for a fraction of a second I see your face.

She is sleeping soundly now, the wet slits of her eyelids not quite meeting in a glint of white, the irises moving underneath, towards whatever it is babies dream of. She won't wake. I go downstairs. I put your tape into the machine and the music rises to the beamed ceiling.

> O, nuit profonde
> Qui tient le monde
> Dans le remords plongé . . .

Such a terrible recording, the words almost impossible to hear, barely comprehensible, sung by foreigners. A world between your existence and mine now, the whole dark expanse of the Atlantic. The pints of blood I lost. The pints of blood that remain.

And Hannah. In my mind's eye her small image holds steady. Funny little thing. Funny monkey. Where did she come from? Her unfocused eyes that open to the small hours and see nothing – a blur of smile, a nipple – and are satisfied. Her heavy head bobbing. Her rooting mouth. Where did she really come from? Would you have killed her, really? Could you take her in your arms and wish us both dead?

Now you've gone I can tell you anything I like and you don't have to listen. I can reel off all the extenuating circumstances one by one, and you can't stop me, you can't answer back. I can tell you exactly how it began to go wrong between us, or where that first touch really came from. I can tell you things about Hannah, details you would never be patient enough to listen to in the flesh. I can try to make you understand, finally, as if understanding were still something to believe in. Let me start by telling you about Steve.

Steve was kind. Kind. Something you wouldn't know much about. And I was *lonely*. Do you even know what that means? To find yourself completely on your own in a foreign city you've never even been to before? All those earnest little visits to the *Syndicat d'Initiative*, all those glossy little leaflets full of ads for plush restaurants and three-star hotels. Visiting flaky old churches. Looking at amateurish displays of photographs from the last war. Trying to take them in. Do you realise those pictures were almost the first thing I saw when I got here? It was either that, or back to my sordid little room.

And we knew each other already, I think I must have told you that much. We came from the same university. He was in his second year, I was a research student. I remembered him, vaguely. He was one of a crowd in the buttery, sitting over pints and telling jokes. Their table used to rock suddenly to a storm of laughter, and I would know that the joke had been something obscene.

But I'd always quite liked him. In spite of his fair, reddish face and light hair. In spite of the public school, the military parents in Singapore. I was actually glad when I heard he was going to be an assistant in one of the local *lycées*, while I was a *lectrice* at the university. That night we met again at the AFB party he told some of the dubious jokes to me. And I laughed, as anyone would have. A week later I asked him back to my room.

It was a small room. I never really told you. A student's room at the bottom of a tall apartment block on the outskirts. It had a hard stone floor and the stones used to get hot from the under-floor heating. You could feel it on the soles of your bare feet, like living over a volcano. I had a camping stove, a wash-basin with a single cold tap. Last thing at night I used to leave a bowl of water on the floor to warm up slightly while I was asleep, so that in the morning I could get straight up and wash. Some mornings I used to find the bodies of cockroaches floating. I used to pick them out and wash in the water any-way. Some nights I used to wake up without any reason. That feeling, as if someone was trying to send me some kind of message. I used to turn on the light. And I'd see something out of the corner of my eye, something scuttling along the skirting. They must have had a nest in a dark hole somewhere. Once I woke up and saw one on the wall a few feet over my bed. I thought they were beetles from outside on the street. I hadn't ever seen roaches. Can you believe it? I had to go to the library and look them up. I looked at the illustrations. '*Blatte*,' was what it said. 'Also, *cafard*.' That first night when Steve asked me how I was getting on, that was all I could think of.

Not surprising, really, under the circumstances. '*J'ai le cafard,*' I told him. I'm depressed. That was the first time I remember smiling at anything in that room. That was the first time I began to think I might actually manage to get to like the place.

And Steve was kind. He really was. 'You've got to get out of here,' he said to me. It sounded so bloody pathetic. 'You've got to get yourself out of this somehow.'

'Out of this room?' I remember looking round at the whole sordid 6 by 12 of it, my posters tacked up on the back of the wardrobe, that dark blue flannelette sheet I used to have as a bedspread, the stupid lampshade I'd improvised from orange sugar-paper. And that ludicrously expensive carved candle I bought once in a moment of total madness. I didn't dare light it, it would've been like setting fire to a little wad of ten-franc notes. It got to be quite a joke. I used to tell people I was going to light it the day my first child was five.

'From this city,' was what he said. 'This country.'

'Where can I go? Home?'

And he, fool that he was, just grinned at me. 'Nothing quite that drastic. How about Spain?'

'*Spain?*' I didn't have any car then. Spain was five hundred miles away.

'Why not?'

'How am I going to get there?'

'In the van.' He had a rattling old banger of a Mini with dirt on the floor and rusting sills. 'We get a week off at the end of the month, for *Toussaint.* They spend their time putting bloody chrysanthemums on graves. Is that your idea of a holiday?'

'I'm not sure I ought to . . .'

Don't be so fucking *keen!*' he said. 'Give it a rest. Come with me. We'll drive down the N10, take the road up into the mountains through Andorra. I'll look after you. I'll make sure you feel at home. They probably have even bigger cockroaches there.'

So we went to Spain together, me and Steve, for All Saints. All Souls, in fact, the night we started, driving through the small hours and most of the next day. We only stopped for the occasional cup of coffee or sandwich. And by dusk we were in the hills above Barcelona. He stopped the car in a lay-by and turned off the engine and the headlights. We stared at each other as the light faded. He wrote 'Piss off' backwards in the condensation with his finger. I was too tired even to smile.

We slept in the van, in sleeping-bags. Steve in the back, on the hard flat metal floor. Me across the front seats. Every time I turned over I hit my hip-bone or my knee on the wheel. I tried sleeping the other way round, but then the wheel was frightening, only inches from my face. I woke up every hour or so, shivering, checking the hands of my watch by torchlight. By about six there were ferns of ice at the corners of the windscreen. The sky over the scrubby hills began to turn a faint shade of grey.

We drove down into what seemed to be a small fishing village and bought ourselves coffee in a seedy-looking bar. Our eyes were raw from the night, the day, the night before. Through the thin November sunshine I still kept seeing a blur of red tail-lights. Steve looked bleary, about ten years older. I must have looked just as bad. Then we went and sat on the beach.

It was a pretty unprepossessing beach. Not exactly idyllic. Grey sea beyond grey shingle, and not even much sun either, by that time. I sat down on the hard stones. I clasped my hands round my knees and stared at the waves breaking. Steve flopped down beside me. 'What you need now,' I said to him, 'is one of those handkerchiefs knotted at the corners. That's what you're supposed to wear at the seaside. No self-respecting Englishman is ever without one.'

I remember him laughing. He was kind, I told you. 'Are you coming in? I'm going for a swim.'

'You're crazy! You'll freeze.'

'We're in Spain, for Christ's sake!'

'But it's November! It was below freezing last night. There was ice on the windows.'

'That was up there. Down here it's much warmer.'

'Not that much.'

'Well, anyway. I'm going to try it. Handkerchief, or no handkerchief.' He was starting to strip off. Jacket, pullover, shoes, trousers, shirt. I just sat there. His clothes mounted up on the shingle beside me in an untidy pile.

He was thin. Very white. He made me want to shiver.

'Aren't you going to take your socks off?' I watched him hobble down across the uneven shapes of the stones. I can still see his shoulder-blades jutting suddenly as a sharp edge caught him off balance. He was wearing dark blue underpants. I couldn't keep track of him for long against the dark blue-grey of the sea.

When he came out he was shivering.

'What's it like in there?'

'Bloody cold. You were right. And I haven't got a towel.'

'Jump around,' I told him. 'Wave your arms. Play cricket.'

'I can't play cricket. There's only one of me.'

'Try bowling very slowly and running to the other end before it gets there.' I handed him a piece of driftwood that was lying near my feet. I picked up a round stone and screwed up my eyes. 'Here you are: Thos. Ives, Tonbridge. The best.'

'Arsehole.' He took it from me and ran a few paces towards the sea, bowling in slow motion. It hit the ground a few feet in front of us and rolled on, stopping just short of the waves. He came back to me up the steep slope of the beach. He was still shivering uncontrollably. His teeth were chattering, his white skin was even whiter with cold.

'You're a complete fool, do you know that?' I took off my anorak and the sweatshirt under it. I turned the sweatshirt inside out. Then I went up to him and started rubbing him dry with the fleecy side of the fabric, until the shivering finally stopped.

'Did I ever tell you the one about the woman with the child, and the balloons?' he said.

That was when Steve bought the guitar. 'What the hell do you want a guitar for, anyway?' I asked him. 'Can you play the guitar?'

He looked rueful, stroking his chin. 'Not yet.'

'Are you going to learn?'

'I thought I might.'

It reminded me of my UCCA form. Under 'Interests' I had written, 'I am thinking of learning the cello.' Well, I *was* thinking of it. 'Do you know a teacher? Have you got someone in mind?'

'I'll find someone. Guitar teachers are two a penny in France.'

I probably sighed. I reached in my pocket for my little Spanish phrase-book. But there wasn't a section that had anything at all to do with musical instruments. 'Wouldn't you rather have a hotel room with hot and cold running water and a trouser-press?' I asked him.

The shop was dark after the white sunlight. We came in from the street and found ourselves surrounded by guitars, Spanish, classical, in light wood or dark, with 6 strings or 12, some of them with wonderful designs on them that went all round the hole like dark lace or the petals of a black flower. Amazing. Plectrums on shelves in a glass-fronted cabinet – plastic, or horn, or something half-transparent, I don't know what it was. And those straps they wear over their shoulders. Really strange colour combinations – orange with purple, pink with bright green. Then this old geezer came out. He must have been hiding somewhere at the back of the shop. He looked at us as if we were half-wits.

'*Una guitarra,*' Steve said. '*No cara, pero . . . muy melodiosa.*' I was trying to look as if I wasn't with him, it was too awful. I was pretending to look at the guitars in the window. They were displayed on those plastic support things so that they leaned slightly towards us. All you could really see was the plain wood of the underneath. I remember looking past them, out on to the street, and seeing a young couple walking arm in arm. Her head was tilted towards his shoulder so that her hair swung across her face. 'Be careful,' I said, almost under my breath. 'You don't want to let yourself in for . . .'

But the man had already left us, busying himself somewhere in a smaller room at the back. Then he came forward again. He was carrying something. He put it into Steve's hands. I expected him to start speaking to us, either in broken English or in a flood of Catalan we couldn't have begun to understand, but he didn't say anything. The skin round his eyes was all weathered and crinkled. He watched Steve holding the thing. You could see Steve hadn't got a clue. The old geezer obviously thought we were hilarious. In the end he reached out and took the guitar out of Steve's hands. Then he sat down on a chair in one corner with it on his knee and played a sudden sequence that made the whole shop vibrate. And then a snatch of something quite different. Scarlatti? If you'd been there you would have known what it was. My eyes filled with tears suddenly. It's called lack of sleep. I turned my back for a minute. Finally the old guy stood up and handed the guitar back.

'Not expensive,' he said. 'And not a bad instrument to learn on.' His voice as he said it sounded perfectly English. It was really creepy, somehow. I don't know if you'll understand that. And as he spoke I sort of got the feeling he was really looking at me.

There is no appropriate way for Laurence to visit my house. Whatever she wears, however hard she tries to make concessions, it is never going to be easy for her in this setting. Even her wrists give her away, thin and delicate almost as the anatomy of a bird. I see the bones shift slightly as she moves her hand. It is her right hand, lifted to adjust the strap of her bag across her left shoulder. Her face is lifted too, as she waits for me to open the door of my cottage. She seems to be studying the old stones.

I open it with Hannah in my arms and see Laurence take a step backwards. In spite of everything, she is unprepared. And I am standing there in my shapeless clothes, my body itself still baggy under them, still bleeding, my hair unwashed and greasy. She has never thought about these things.

'Laurence. Come in.' I stand aside and she brushes past me, into the kitchen. She stands looking round her, at the mess of dirty crockery and baby-clothes on the counter, at the fly-paper hanging from the ceiling, already crusted with black bodies. She goes to the window over the sink and looks out, to where the cows stand, a few feet away, their big heads drooping over the fence. I watch a shadow flicker on her wrist as she fingers the strap of her bag.

She looks back at me, over her shoulder. 'I brought you something.'

'How kind of you.'

I show her into the other room, where the mess is less obvious. She sits down in one of the chairs and looks at the blank glass front of the woodstove. I sit down near her and settle Hannah on my knee.

Laurence slips the strap from her shoulder and opens her bag on her lap. She takes out a small parcel wrapped in blue-flowered paper and festooned with narrow corkscrew curls of silver ribbon. Done in the shop with a rasp of the scissors. 'C'est pour offrir?' And a smile.

I open it as best I can with Hannah still in my arms. It's a tiny white cotton shirt with pin-tucks at the collar. On the crisp little pocket there is a stylised boat embroidered in red and blue. 'Oh, how delightful!' I tell her. 'And how kind.'

'There's a card.' For once she looks faintly embarrassed. 'Did you see the card?'

I slit the envelope clumsily, across the limp weight of Hannah's small body. A tasteful cradle, the curtains gathered over it with a pink bow, the baby itself invisible. Inside they have all signed it – Laurence's own flourish of a signature, Paul and Mireille, Francis, Lervain's small neat name in the bottom right-hand corner. 'All good things for you and for the child,' Mireille has written in English. She has even added a kiss. 'It's very kind of you,' I say again. 'Of every-one. Will you thank them all when you see them? And I'll write, of course.'

'They won't expect you to.' Laurence looks round the room. 'They know how busy you must be . . . now.'

I shift Hannah to my other arm. Her body makes some kind of subterranean rumble. 'And how are they all?'

'They're all off for the summer. All going their separate ways now, until October. I saw Paul the other day. They'd finished, more or less. He was just coming out of the first-year prose meeting. They had to set the *moyenne* extra high this year, he said, or too many people would have passed.'

It seems like another world. 'And you?' I say. 'How are things for you?'

'Oh, me . . .' She shrugs. The smooth shoulders rise and settle again. Stretching her wings. 'Still time as metaphor in the last plays. You know. There's *so much*! But I love it.'

'Is Lervain helpful?'

'Oh . . .' She looks down, playing with the metal strap of her watch, stretching it from her wrist and letting it spring back with a little snap. 'It's ironic. Time. Always more time. That's what I need.'

'Will they give you more?'

'Oh . . . yes. Time, if you like. But the way to buy the time, that's the problem. What I really need is an assistantship. To help me finish. Lervain knows that.'

'Can't he come up with something?'

The watchstrap narrows as it stretches. I flinch as it hits her wrist. 'He might. He's been talking to someone. He told me. He said funding might be available. If I . . .' She turns her face to the window. The cows have gone now, grouped in a pool of shadow under the tree on the far side of the field. The fence is slightly broken where they come and hang their heads over it every morning. 'If he feels he can make a really strong case. But his position's rather delicate. And he's very scrupulous.'

'What about Francis? Can't he speak up for you?'

'Oh, Francis!' She says it impatiently. 'Francis has his own ideas. And anyway . . .'

'I thought perhaps you were one of those ideas.'

She laughs, but it sounds almost angry. 'Oh yes.' She stands up suddenly, and the expensive wrapping-paper slides to the floor. 'For a while this last year, so did I.'

I go with her to the door. We both blink at the light. The late morning is full of farm sounds, the smell of warm hedgerows and silage, the outdoors. She kisses me on both cheeks, an unreal kiss, an apology. Only the light touch of her cheek, first on one side of my face, then on the other. She turns and walks quickly towards her car, parked beside mine on the gravel. I am struck by how clean it is.

She climbs in and rolls down the window. As she drives past my door she slows almost to a stop and waves. I lift Hannah's little closed fist and wave it back. Hannah startles and opens her eyes. Then she coughs up a flood of half-digested milk into the hollow at the base of my neck.

I have one last pile of *maîtrise* assignments to mark and give back before I can allow myself to be free of the year. They are stacked up on a wooden chest, under the window in the downstairs room, sun streaming across them, patterned with waving leaf-shadows from outside. As soon as Hannah is asleep after her early morning feed I make myself a bowl of coffee and sit down with them. The pile is on the low white wicker table at my elbow. About ten of them, translations into English. I take up my pen and start on the first sheet.

Outside I can hear birds, a cat mewing, the ducks calling for their breakfast. And Dominique banging her kitchen door and rattling something in a bowl, calling. I leaf through the assignments one by one until I get to Marthe's.

It is scrawled in her large untidy handwriting. A blot that is smudged at one corner where her pen leaked and her sleeve brushed over the page. An almost indecipherable word that might or might not be a mistake. A *faute rédhibitoire,* even – something almost too shameful to underline. I work through it steadily, sighing, wishing she would let herself be clearer, wishing I could be more generous. I find that, try as I might, I can't possibly give it more than 12 out of 20. Not that she will care.

I put it back, lifting the pile and slipping her exercise in at the bottom. And then something drops out, a small piece of paper with a torn top edge where the coil of wire joined it to the notebook, the paper teeth irregular and jagged, a thin strip of perforated paper still dangling. It is some kind of list.

It seems to be a list of complaints, of a teacher's many failings. 'Lack of clarity about aims and objectives,' it begins. 'Confused ideological basis.' 'Inadequate feedback.' It occurs to me that the failings are my own, and that most of them are justified. 'Favouritism,' it ends.

'*Favouritism?*' I start to think back. Have I ever shown any evidence at all of favouritism in that class? Do I have any favourites, in fact? And if I did, wouldn't Marthe herself be one of them? And if she were, would that in itself be grounds for complaint?

I crumple the little note up in the palm of my hand. I stand up and go to the window. Out in the yard, Dominique is walking backwards and forwards, doing something in the garden. She has a watering-can in her hand. She turns back towards me to water the hanging baskets on the wall, just where the end of the farmhouse becomes the wall of my cottage. She doesn't see me. I step back away from the window, into the shadow of the room.

'Lack of clarity about aims . . .' Yes, that certainly. And the suspect ideology too. But the lack of feedback, when I have given them so much, spent so many unseen hours poring over their work, with something almost like love? I have been so conscientious. Even Lervain has said so. Could I have done more? And *favouritism*? The word sticks in my throat. Who did I ever favour, in that class? Come on, Marthe, tell me. Who did I ever encourage or even smile at, if not the ones I was afraid of allowing myself to like least?

I fetch my pad and a pen and start to write her a reply. 'Thank you for giving me such a useful and detailed criticism of my teaching style and practices, and for your honesty,' it begins. 'You've given me so much to think about, both for the past year and for the future.' I sit chewing the top of my pen, wondering how it ought to end.

Two days later I am just washing up the lunch dishes when I see her car coming down the lane towards me. She drives round to the gravel and parks. I hear a loud hammering on my kitchen door. I turn and see her through the glass.

She is actually holding my letter in her hand. She waves it in front of my face. 'This is all a misunderstanding,' she says.

'Yes?' I wait for her to explain. Is she going to tell me that the list referred to some other teacher, that it didn't implicate me at all? 'I thought you wanted me to know just what you thought of me,' I say.

'No.' The letter is less obvious now. The hand that held it almost to my face has settled back at her side, the piece of paper drooping from it, forgotten. 'It was true. It was all true – as you recognised. But you weren't meant to see it. You were the very last person I wanted to see it. I'm sorry.'

'Who did you want to see it?' In the warm light of early summer I feel cold suddenly. Francis? Lervain? What price my chances of staying on here then? 'What were you trying to do, exactly?' I ask her.

I gesture towards the kitchen bench, its worn cushions blotched with damp from the wall. But she shakes her head. 'I wrote it for myself, to clarify . . .'

'Your own aims and objectives?'

She laughs. I have never seen her so angry.

I say in my softest, most English voice, 'I really am grateful. You've helped me put my finger on some of what was wrong with that class. I've always felt it. That group was always uncomfortable. I wasn't sure why. Now I know.'

She is glaring at me.

'Now I can do better next year. I'll be able to think hard about all this over the summer. And then perhaps in October . . .'

She looks at me. She reaches down and folds my letter up again, in its original creases. She slides it into the back pocket of her jeans. 'I won't be in the class in October,' she says.

I raise my eyebrows. 'Oh . . .'

'I'm thinking of transferring. Moving to Paris. I've got friends there. And this place is so provincial. The teaching's so pathetic. They never get anyone who's any good.'

'So it's not just me?' I say drily.

But she doesn't let me off the hook. 'Oh, well, you're the worst. But the others aren't famous, either.'

'I never wanted to be famous. I only wanted to do it right.'

'Oh . . .' She laughs again, that same laugh. 'You're doing it right. Don't worry. They love you. Lervain, all of them. *La petite doctoresse.* I've heard them. He loves you.'

I want to hit her. She is standing with her back to the wall. Before I know what I am doing, my two arms are extended, my two hands flat on the cold stones, one on either side of her head. She turns her face to one side.

And then I see it is useless. There is no common ground between us. There is nothing at all that I could say, that wouldn't be misinterpreted. We live in two different countries, speak two separate languages. She is forcing me to hate her, and eventually I will.

When she has gone, I am left alone with Hannah. I let myself sink down on to the stained cushions of the kitchen bench and lean forward, my elbows on the table, my face in my hands. The kitchen door isn't shut properly. The latch rattles against the wood of the frame.

I get up and shut it, too hard, almost hard enough to break

45

the glass. After the crash I hear Hannah's small voice rise, somewhere above the kitchen. A single wail, to begin with. Then a steady complaint, regular as breathing. And then the oddly impersonal rasp of some human machine.

I bring her down and get ready to give her her bath. I lay her on her changing mat on the counter as I fill the kitchen sink with warm water. I roll up my sleeves and test the temperature with my elbow.

I undress her and soap her all over. I lather her hair, the almost invisible line where the soft peak of down meets the skin of her forehead, still flaking slightly from the clinic. The thin drum of the fontanelle, beating under my thumb.

I lay her in the water, my right hand under the back of her neck to grip her small right arm, my left hand free to trickle a thin stream of suds over her with the sponge. Her body is like a frog's, the belly swollen and almost shapeless, the ugly knot of umbilicus still protruding, the scraggy end of brownish skin still fastened with surgical tape. And her face is like a frog's, too, barely human, the jowls slack and froglike, as if she were listening with some hidden inner ear, listening to the sensation of the water on her body. She kicks her wrinkled legs, and splashes me. I reach up with my free hand and wipe the water out of my eye.

But when I get her out she starts to yell again. As if she couldn't bear to be lifted from the water, as if water were her only home. As I try to pat her dry with the towel her whole spine goes rigid, her thin legs extended, straight and stiff under my hands. And as I dry her I am crying too, the tears suddenly streaming down my face – for Laurence, for Lervain, for Marthe, for the crumpled note with its list of my inadequacies, the true story of my life. And you are not here. From where you are you are unaware even that you have a daughter, you can't hear either of us.

There is a loud knocking at the kitchen door and I turn round. Dominique is standing there, her mouth opening and closing on the other side of the glass. I brush the tears quickly from my cheeks with a corner of the towel and let her in, Hannah still screaming, clutched to my shoulder in a warm, damp package.

'My God! What's going on in here? Are you murdering

her, or what?' Her voice is gruff, but her eyes are kind, taking it all in, the splashes of water on the counter, the open bottle of shampoo, Hannah's face like an over-ripe tomato, her blotched limbs escaping from the folds and waving with frustration. Her sea-anemone fingers.

'Yes,' I say. 'I was killing her. Evidently. And in between I was trying to give her a bath.'

Dominique looks at me shrewdly. She has seen my red eyes, the dark streaks on the front of my shirt where the water has run down. 'Or she was killing you. Which was it?'

She is kind. My eyes fill with tears again. It would be all right, if only people didn't try to be kind to me. I can't say anything.

'Here.' She reaches out for Hannah and I put the package in her arms.

I lean across them both to rip a couple of sheets of kitchen towel from the roll on its holder by the window. I blow my nose hard and wipe my eyes. 'I'm sorry.' I blow my nose a second time.

'*Sorry?* What the hell for?'

'For letting her make all this noise. For disturbing you. For being a bad mother,' I say.

'Rubbish.' She is rocking Hannah now in her arms and the crying has subsided. There is only the odd shudder. 'Pass me her clothes.' I hand her the vest, the nappy, the Babygro. I watch her unroll Hannah on her lap and dust her with powder. She coaxes her gently into the little garments, one by one, wriggling her own hands into the holes and feeding Hannah's arms through. It looks so simple. When Hannah is fully dressed Dominique gives her back to me and stands up to clear away the things – the lotion, baby shampoo, the pile of small clothes on the floor, soaked with urine. She goes over to the sink and pulls the plug. 'Is this where you bath her all the time?'

'Yes.'

'Haven't you got a proper bath for her?'

'No.'

'Why didn't you tell me?'

'I didn't think it mattered.'

'No.' She hangs the towel over the makeshift line suspended

from a beam over our heads. Then she holds out her arms for Hannah again and I give her back. 'It doesn't matter. Not to the baby, anyway. It's what my mother always did, when we were kids. But it's not very convenient for you. A proper baby bath would make your life easier.'

'Oh . . .' I don't know what to say to her. 'There hasn't been much time. It's only a week since I got out of the clinic. I haven't really managed to get myself organised. I'm still catching up with all my work.'

She looks suddenly sceptical. 'Of course,' she says. 'The work.' She turns Hannah round so that their faces are close together. She leans forward and rests her chin on my baby's downy head, looking at me over the top of it. Hannah looks like some strange hairy growth in her neck. I want to smile, but she is looking at me seriously. 'Don't you call Hannah work?' she asks me. 'What do you call this, then?' She has no free hand to wave. She leans forward and uses her eyes to indicate the far corners of the room, the fly-swatter on its nail, the full bucket in its slopped puddle on the tiled floor. 'Recreation?'

It is the evening. Hannah is in her cot, finally, making only the occasional whimper. I tiptoe out of the room and go downstairs.

Am I hungry? Thirsty? I don't know any more. Apart from the tiredness, the slight soreness from the stitches, my own body might not exist. Apart from the dragging feeling in my belly when I feed her, the sudden pricking of my nipples whenever she cries.

But once she is asleep I am non-existent. It is almost restful. I could stop eating and drinking now for ever, like some saint.

But on my way downstairs I catch sight of Dominique again. She is walking past the side window, with something large and white in her arms. She taps on my glass as she goes past and gesticulates to me to open the door to her.

'Well, this is it.' She pushes past me and puts the thing down on the table. 'Every comfort. Now you'll have to cry about something else, both of you.'

'Where did it come from?'

'It was mine. For the grandchildren, when they came. But they're all past that now. I don't need it.'

48

'It's . . . very white.'

'I cleaned it up for you.'

'You're right.' I smile at her suddenly. 'Soon there won't be anything to cry about.'

'Not Hannah, anyway. She's adorable. And not work, either. Tell them you're a mother now. Tell them you don't give a damn about it, their work.'

'They know.'

'Well, you tell them. And don't worry about the crying. All new mothers cry. It's normal.' She pats me on the shoulder. Then she leaves. When she has gone I turn out the kitchen light and go back into the other room. Through the open doorway I can still see the bath gleaming, the white plastic scrubbed so clean it is almost luminous. I imagine it full of water, the little waves lapping at the brim and running over, the students' end-of-year assignments folded into paper boats.

'On days like this,' Paul is saying, 'you could almost believe in divine Providence. Or at least, that something out there is taking a rest.'

'Oh, my poor darling.' Mireille is lying in the grass next to him. She reaches up and runs her hand through his hair, against its natural growth, making it stand up on end, a younger man's crew-cut. He looks vaguely comical, the wire-framed half-moon glasses slipping down the bridge of his nose. 'Are you so overworked?' She sighs. 'The end of the year. It's always the same thing.'

I am lying on my back too, on my old coat, thrown down on a bed of grass and cowslips, Hannah in the borrowed carry-cot at my elbow. I squint up at the sun through waving leaves and see it change, a sudden spear of light, then a quite different pattern, a complicated pinkish star filtered through my eyelashes. The leaves above me shift in the breeze and it changes again. 'Don't take any notice of me,' Paul is saying. 'I'm always like this at this time of year. Grumpy. Exhausted. And it passes. It always passes.'

I sit up to look into the carry-cot. Hannah is asleep, the cellular blanket up round her ears. A cherub. Around me they are talking again, sharing out food and wine. 'And have you managed to find somewhere to live?' Mireille is saying.

49

The new woman is called Helen. She's tall and dark, with wavy hair that falls over her shoulders. And she has a young child. She doesn't say much, stricken with shyness in this odd gathering arranged partly for her benefit. She glances over in my direction. 'Oh . . . I've got time yet. I haven't got the money to pay a lot of wasted rent in advance. I'm just here to have a quick look round, to sort things out for Chryssa. There'll be time for all that later, I'm sure.' She looks at me again, as if for corroboration.

'It's no use looking at me,' I say. 'I'm not very proficient at that kind of thing, even on my own account.' Then I hear myself saying, 'But I'll be here, if you need help.' I reach into the carry-cot and make a show of rearranging the covers.

'That's very nice of you.' She looks round at us all – Paul and Mireille, me, Laurence. 'I'll remember that. And I'll re-member this. Thanks.'

Paul puts his empty wine-glass down and it falls over on the grass, the new green blades squashed against its side. He yawns. 'This is no good, though,' he says. He gets up suddenly and goes over to the car. He opens the boot and takes something out, a dirty white disc. A plate? But he flicks his wrist and it floats towards us through the sun, veering suddenly as the wind catches it, and wobbling to earth in a patch of shadow under trees on the low side of the field. He grins and shrugs, plodding down to fetch it. He bends over and straightens up again. We hear his voice faintly, '*Chryssa! Attrape!*' He feints and tries to catch her eye, but she has hidden behind Helen, nervous at hearing her own name in the strange accent. He calls again, this time in English. 'Hey, Chryssa! For you! Catch!'

Helen tries to haul her out from among the folds of her long skirt, but Chryssa resists, clinging to her mother's legs fiercely, her head burrowed into the dark. The mother is stroking the child's head. 'Don't be so silly. It's only a frisbee. Look! You can see where it goes. Wait till it lands and then run and get it for him. No one will be looking at you. No one's going to laugh.'

But Chryssa still clings, hanging her head, swinging on her mother's legs as if they were two posts, holding on tight. I watch them for a moment. They make a lovely picture, the two of them, the mother's skirts blowing against sunlight and the hollow in the child's nape a small pool of shadow. In a minute she will start to cry.

I walk away from them down towards the stream. I sit on a stone on the bank, my feet on a brown mulch of dead hawthorn and horse chestnut leaves. I look up, but there is only a net of fine hawthorn twigs meeting over the water. The big hands of horse chestnut must have blown here during the winter from somewhere else.

I sit watching the water, combed over the stones, catching the light. Near my feet there is a dark pool, deeper, hollowed out by the past months of rain. I can see clearly to the bottom, the layered lining of black leaves rotting slowly into silt. Bubbles rising. Perhaps there are even fish.

I hear a noise behind me and look up, over my shoulder. It is Mireille, stumbling through deep grass at the top of the bank. She parts the hawthorn branches and sits down beside me, sucking at one finger where a thorn has caught her skin. 'You haven't really told me.' She smiles, her pleasant open face expecting an answer. 'I want to hear about it all, the whole story.' I can see the wrinkles at the corners of her eyes.

'Oh . . .' The pool reflects us, the twin dark humps of our bodies, our heads reaching down into darkness. 'There's not much to tell. What did you want to know?'

'Everything. How it was. How it went. If you suffered.' She laughs, but the questions are serious.

'I don't know. I haven't got anything to measure it against. It was all pretty ordinary, as far as I could gather. I don't know if I suffered. How can you tell?'

'What a very English answer!' She is looking at me now in amusement. 'Well, did it hurt?'

'I think so. I don't remember. Yes.'

'Laurence said they had to use forceps.'

'If Laurence said it . . .' I say. 'Don't you think she's reliable?'

'But I wanted to have it . . . *from the horse's mouth.*' She says it in English. 'You know, we were all very concerned about you. Everyone. If there's anything we can do to help . . .'

Something breaks the surface of the water. A stickleback?

51

'I'm fine,' I say. 'I think. And I've got time now to get myself together. I'll get it all sorted out by October, the childcare, the work, everything. It couldn't have been timed better. And next year I'll be able to make a fresh start.'

'You're very courageous.' She picks up a handful of dry crumbling stuff and lets it trickle through her fingers. 'Have you told Joseph, at least?'

It's very quiet. From here we can't hear the others' voices. Only the noise of the water as it runs into the pool, over the faces of the rocks. 'I didn't think he would want to know.'

'Well, that's up to you, of course.' She is standing up now, brushing the dirt from the seat of her trousers. 'But if you were me . . . And Paul.'

'Joseph's not Paul,' I tell her. 'He's a lot younger than Paul. And he's got his life.'

'Hmmm.' She reaches out for my hand and pulls, until I am standing beside her in a tangle of spiky hawthorns. For the first time I notice that they are full of blossom. We push them aside and step through them, into the open. 'And what about you? Haven't you got your life?' she says.

They are quiet now. One by one all the voices have sunk to a murmur, and the silence of the woods and fields has re-established itself, the small sounds of the birds and the leaves and the water louder than the human sounds of our picnic. Laurence is lying on her stomach, her head in her arms, asleep, probably. An ant makes its laborious way across one slim ankle. Mireille is reading. Paul has found a straw hat from somewhere, the brim pulled down in front to shade his eyes. He is doing an English crossword. From time to time he looks up over the rim of his glasses and frowns at the light moving over the grass. Off to one side, Helen has taken Chryssa on her lap to look at a picture-book. I hear her low voice as she repeats the text, the child's voice raised in some question. Then the sleepy monotone continues.

They all look up at Hannah's sharp cry. Feeding time. I feel the sudden sharp pricking in my nipples and a sticky sensation as the milk starts to leak out. I grab her out of the carry-cot and hoist her to my shoulder. 'We're just going for a short walk,' I tell them.

I go down to the stream and push through the bushes, at the same place. I shield Hannah's face with my hand.

Together we follow the water, my fingers curled round the back of her small head. I take it slowly, because the bank is uneven and steep and I am afraid of falling with her in my arms. I look at my own feet, picking their way among the roots and slippery grasses, but in my mind's eye I can see her face, the eyes wide and half unseeing, staring backwards into a blur of green light.

She has found her fist now. Next to my ear I can hear a rhythmic sucking louder than the rush and gurgle of the stream. I hug her closer. I recognise every inch of her, the feel and smell of her skin, as if it were my own. She is warm against my neck.

At one point the stream widens and gets shallower, making a flat pool where the water-boatmen dart. A dragonfly hovers over the surface, a bluish blur of wings. Someone has thought to make stepping-stones to the other side, big footprints in the stream, just close enough together for us to walk across them without fear. One or two of them are still half-submerged, but I manage to cross to the other side without getting my feet wet.

And the field on the other side is extraordinary, a whole wide expanse of waving cowslips. Not just the few scattered flowers we found at our picnic spot, but a thick yellow tide of them, like ghee, swilling over the tipped meadow. And everywhere the bees are moving between the small trumpets. The whole field of flowers seems to be giving out a shared hum, as if the sound is coming, not from any one bee, or even from a swarm of bees, but from the warmth of the sun itself, as if the yellow colour has been translated into something audible that only Hannah and I are aware of. I sit down carefully and unbutton my blouse. I turn her so that she is comfortable against me and give her my breast, wincing as she finds it. Then there is only the hum and the little voiced sigh she makes to punctuate each mouthful, as the cowslips close in behind us, the grass springing up blade by blade in my footprints so that no one can follow us or find us. And we can stay here for ever. I can learn to keep myself alive on a diet of roots and berries. Hannah will grow plump and healthy on my milk.

And they will search for us without ever finding us. None of them will be able to tell which way we have gone.

Something wakes me – a cloud, blotting out the sunlight for a moment, falling on our faces as a colder shadow. She is asleep beside me, her face close to mine, the grass tickling her skin. She sneezes. I watch her slip back into the dream. Then she startles suddenly, for no apparent reason, head back and her four small limbs jerking outwards in that odd reflex of the newborn. Soon she will outgrow it. I squint up at the sun.

The little cloud has moved on now, small and backlit, white wings or streaming hair. I try to conjure it into the shape of a cherub, but it isn't quite right: there is an odd protruberance at the lower left-hand edge, a wisp of cloud that is neither foot nor wing-tip. Others are coming up behind it over the horizon. I roll over and get to my knees, letting them all go. I crouch in the grass and pick a bunch of cowslips. So many of them, the hairs of their long pinkish stems warm in my hand. Even without moving my feet from this one position I have a large bunch of them, enough to fill a vase.

Hannah is asleep. I can see the whites of her eyes, where her eyelids aren't quite closed. I can see the shape of her irises moving under the veil of skin. I pick her up, very gently, not waking her, wrapping the shawl round her to hold her to-gether. Together we make our way back.

The stream is somehow not the same in this direction. I follow it back the way I came, against the flow of the water, slightly uphill. It runs and trickles to meet me, the stones near the bank coated with moss and slime, the flat pools cloudy with silt. The dragonfly has gone now. Somehow I miss the shallow place with the stepping-stones and find myself level with our picnic spot on the wrong side. I can see the colours through the leaves, the flash of bright lettering on Mireille's paperback, a navy triangle that must be the side of the carry-cot, the deep pink of Laurence's cotton sweater, rolled into a neat pillow under her head.

From here I have no idea how I am going to cross the water. I try to remember how far downstream the place with the stepping-stones was, but it is hard to picture it exactly. In memory I can see only my own feet, picking their way among the slippery growth of the bank, my face lowered to avoid overhanging branches, Hannah's head bobbing on my shoulder through the dappled green.

The stream isn't so wide – somewhere between two and three feet. And not that deep either, perhaps only a foot at the edges. But the bank itself is steep, almost sheer. Impossible to get any purchase. I imagine my feet landing and slipping away from me, my hands tied. From the bank opposite me I seem to hear a chorus of voices from my childhood. 'Come on, Sarah, jump! You can do it! Come on.' The remembered faces cluster under the hawthorns, grouped in encouragement, only faintly scornful. Perhaps I can do it. Perhaps I can. But there is Hannah, a small precious weight on my shoulder. I have Hannah to think about now.

I won't be flustered. I sit down beside the water to weigh up the alternatives.

And it is then that I hear the voices, floating towards me, piercing the green web, as clear as if the stream itself had suddenly shrivelled to late summer, exposing the lines of its bed. And laughter. Between the exchanges they are laughing at someone. I hardly even have to make an effort to hear what it is they are saying. 'And "suspect ideological basis"!' It is Mireille's voice. 'What a wonderfully versatile expression that is! I wish someone would say that to *me*!'

'And it actually used the word "favouritism".' Paul's voice now, explaining. I can imagine him spreading his hands, the gesture itself a disclaimer, more effective than words. ' "Favouritism"! Like something in a primary school class! Can you credit it?'

'It's so *unfair*, when she's so conscientious, someone so . . . And just now, when she's had so much going on, all this other business to put up with. And quite alone, if you think about it. Only her own resources to fall back on. I'd like to get my hands on them, whoever it was!'

Paul gives a short laugh. 'Not easy.'

Then Laurence's voice, cool and musical. 'Who do you think it was?'

'God knows! I shouldn't have thought she could possibly have made any enemies. Would you, Mireille?'

'Everyone likes her. Everyone's sympathetic. But something

obviously happened, in that *maîtrise* group. She must have wounded someone's sensibilities, to lay herself open to something like this.'

I don't want to hear any more. I bury my head in Hannah's warm bundle of shawl, but the words still filter through to me. I can't help hearing them.

'Will it make any difference, do you think? Has Lervain got wind of it?'

Laurence says, 'He's very scrupulous.'

'Whatever that means,' Paul says.

There is a silence. Then Mireille says again, 'Does he know?'

Against my cheek Hannah stirs slightly, wriggling her arms free of the shawl. I kiss her forehead and she goes still.

'And Francis?'

Again there is a slight hesitation. I try to imagine their faces, Mireille's concerned, faintly indignant, Paul's matter-of-fact. But it is Laurence who answers. 'Francis usually seems to know everything.'

'Well, tell him from me . . .' The sound of Mireille's voice is different, louder. She must have turned round to speak to Laurence directly. 'Tell him from me it's a joke, all this. An accident. It could have been any one of us.'

'My own immediate objective being always only to placate my wife.' Their good-natured laughter comes to me on the slight breeze, through Hannah's feathery hair.

Perhaps if I close my eyes I can cross it. At worst I will only make a fool of myself, emerging dripping and apologetic in their midst, Hannah still screaming at the sudden jolt. But I keep my eyes open.

And it is easy. It is like flying. For a moment the two of us are airborne, suspended over water, the hair on both our heads lifting like wings. My right foot hits the far bank and falls back, grazing the surface. But my left has found a flat place. For a split second I totter, pulled backwards by Hannah's weight, but then we right ourselves. We have come across unscathed. The indigo canvas of my right shoe is stained darker along one edge where it slipped into the stream, but otherwise we are safe and dry. We've made it. Only the bunched cowslips have really suffered, their stalks a bruised pink mess in my hand. I open my fingers but the stems still cling to my palm. I turn back towards the water and hold my hand out over it. I shake the flowers free and they fall into the current. I watch them float away from me – a bunched clump, then a few last stragglers pulled into alignment by the water. I watch the last one as it is carried off to one side in an eddy, turning lazily through ninety degrees before the current picks it up again. Further down it snags on a rock and hangs there for a good two minutes, the small yellow trumpets half submerged, before it finally capitulates and slides over the edge.

They look up as we emerge from the bushes. A shower of hawthorn petals falls from my fringe on to the top of Hannah's head. I blink. Then I brush it off. Laurence looks at me, taking me in, the rain of falling May-blossom, the wet mark on my shoe. 'Did you have a pleasant walk?'

'Hannah was hungry. I didn't want to embarrass you.'

'Don't be so silly!' Mireille pats the grass next to where she is sitting. 'We wouldn't have minded.' She looks at Paul. 'It wouldn't have been the first time.'

'Madonna, and Child,' Laurence says.

I look at her, trying to work out whether or not the remark is as hostile as it sounds, but she looks away.

'We were just talking of you, actually.'

'Nothing you couldn't have heard,' Mireille says quickly. 'Just about that business. That difficult student you had.'

It is a relief now to lay Hannah down in the carry-cot. She seems to fall asleep instantly. I sit down in the place Mireille has saved for me, smoothing the fabric of my trousers over my knees. The dark patch on my shoe is fading already, its edges shrinking back in the bright sun. 'I wasn't aware that it was common knowledge.'

'Whoever it was sent a note to Paul. With a copy of the one they gave you.'

'Oh.'

'We thought it was hilarious.'

'Did you.'

'Didn't you?'

'No. Actually I thought it was pretty close to the truth.'

'Oh, Sarah, come on!' Mireille leans and puts her arm round

57

me, laughing. 'It was absurd! You mustn't let them dictate terms to you like that.'

'I went through the grievances point by point. They seemed to me to be more or less true,' I say again. 'My ideological basis *is* shaky. My aims and objectives *are* ill-defined.'

'And do you have favourites?' Paul looks up at me, his pen suspended over the crossword.

'No. I'm not guilty of that one. Just Hannah.' I glance over to where she is, only a small patch of skin visible. 'And that's allowed. That's why I had her, I think. And Joseph, of course. I suppose he was my favourite, until he left.'

For a moment the greens and golds of the field melt into a blur. Too bright. I close my eyes. Is it still dark where you are? 'You shouldn't worry,' Mireille is saying.

I open my eyes again. The meadow with its waving grasses is the same as it was, only clearer. The colourful paraphernalia of our picnic is littered all round us. 'I try not to,' I say.

'I don't suppose it's reached Lervain. And if it hasn't . . .'

Paul lays down his paper. 'I certainly won't be the one to tell him.'

Laurence gives a little cough, behind her hand. 'Anyway,' she says, 'he likes you. He's got plans for you. Francis told me. He wants to keep you here. He'll make sure the money's forthcoming from somewhere.'

'Right.' I look over towards the stream, where the hawthorns meet in a green fountain, clotted with blossom, hiding the water.

At the edge of our group Helen stands up. She brushes something from her skirt, a blade of grass or an insect. 'I'm not sure I really want to be a part of all this,' she says. 'It doesn't sound very kind.'

Laurence looks at her. 'Is that why you came here? For kindness?'

'Well, I . . .'

'It's a much underrated quality,' Paul says. 'Something that doesn't come that easily to us sometimes. Something you English are very good at.'

'Aren't I kind to you?' Mireille reaches over and ruffles his hair.

'Well, you're an anglophile. That's why I married you.'

'I'm not sure we're kind.' My own voice sounds gentle and yet somehow exasperated, like my mother's. 'Inhibited, possibly. I keep thinking that one of these days I might just find out that I'm not kind at all.'

But Helen is hardly listening. She is nervous suddenly, shivering. She pulls her cardigan round her shoulders. 'I'm sorry. I didn't mean to start this. It was stupid.'

'Are you all right?' Mireille's voice is full of concern.

'Yes. Of course I am. It's just . . .' She has gone pale. 'And when I get back I have to . . .'

'You've been wearing yourself out. And we've been so rude, talking shop all the time, frightening you with gossip. Poor Helen! What a welcome!' Already she is picking things up from the grass, stacking the plates in the cooler, shaking out rugs and folding them, collecting the empty wine bottles.

Chryssa has wandered off, towards the road. Mireille runs to catch up with her and take her hand. We see her bend over the little girl and say something in her ear. As we catch up with them we begin to decipher it. Mireille is speaking French. '*Tu viens avec nous, dans la voiture? C'est d'accord?*' She is trying to take Chryssa's hand.

But Chryssa has escaped from her. She runs to Helen. She hides her face against Helen's body, clinging so tightly that Helen can't walk. The two of them stop in the middle of the field as we hold our bags and bundles and wait for them to catch up.

And then Chryssa breaks away from her mother and runs to where we are, shouting something at us in what seems to be an unknown language. It is incomprehensible. We look at one another, amused, nonplussed. But then we begin to make out words. 'I won't talk stupid French. *I won't!* And if she says French I won't hear it. I can't hear what you're saying. You make my ears hurt. I want to go *home!*'

But Helen has run to catch up with her and grabbed her by the shoulders. She doesn't say anything. She squats down in the grass and pulls Chryssa across her knee. Then she smacks her hard on the top of her leg. I see tears glinting at the corners of her own eyes. As she sets Chryssa upright again in the field I watch the red shape of her hand rise on the little girl's pale skin like a developing photograph.

59

3

For a while there Steve and I were almost inseparable. I used to walk through the dark streets at night, to his room at the *lycée*. The caretaker used to shine his torch in my face and give me a sort of gruff greeting. Or sometimes Steve would walk to mine. The cockroaches were less in evidence. Someone had told me how to get rid of them. There was some poisonous yellow stuff I used to scatter round the skirting and under the slit of the door. My books and papers, my plate and bowl, my hairbrush, you should have seen it all. Everything was covered with yellow dust.

And he was kind. I told you. We used to have a laugh. He used to tell me jokes to cheer me up. He used to go through his whole repertoire and then start again at the beginning. I must have been an amazing audience. I never remembered the punchlines. He could tell me the same joke over and over again, and I never ever remembered. But one day when he came he was with someone.

'This is Vic. He's a friend, assistant at the *lycée technique*. We met a couple of weeks ago.'

'Great,' I said. 'Welcome.'

Vic was small and dark, with greasy hair and an old donkey-jacket that looked as if it had been picked from the top of a half-lit bonfire. It still smelled of smoke.

Steve looked at me. He looked at my room, the subdued orange lighting, the pictures on the wardrobe, the gold dust. 'I thought, with three of us, we could play cards now,' he said.

'But I don't know how to play cards. Only Snap and Beat Jack Out of Doors. And Old Maid.'

'I'll teach you.' I remember him glancing across at Vic on the other side of my table. It wasn't quite a wink. He got out a battered pack and started to shuffle. The cards were sticky, broken and bent at the corners. 'Three-card Brag? Pontoon?'

'Something easy,' I said. 'Something I'll be able to grasp.'

And that first night, can you believe it, what we ended up

playing was Cheat. We played it into the small hours. I knew they were laughing at me. I knew they both thought I could only be transparently innocent or transparently cunning. My score was totally pathetic. And that seemed to make them laugh even harder. After a while it started to get to me. After a couple of hours I was beginning to wish they would just get up and leave, take the stupid cards out of my room and just piss off. I must have been close to tears. 'What you need is a bit of the strong stuff.' I caught him glancing across knowingly at Vic again.

He went over to where they'd thrown their things across my bed, and rummaged in that ex-army rucksack he always carried. He pulled out a bottle of Calvados. 'Here.'

I hadn't got any glasses. I set out the two brown glass coffee bowls with the plastic beaker I kept my toothbrush in. Steve poured a generous slug, and we drank. We looked at one another. He poured again. By the end of the second round I was beginning to feel things weren't quite so bad.

He used to do that special shuffle, the one they do in films. You know. When the cards fall between the dealer's hands in a sort of blurred cascade. There's something a bit mesmerising about it. Something mechanical, too. He split the pack and cut one half into the other, with another of his superior looks. I could feel I was almost losing it. 'One last hand?' he said.

And then suddenly, I don't know how, I was doing it right. There I was, laughing when I was honest, straight-faced and earnest when I cheated. Occasionally even a double-bluff. 'Four aces,' I said. I slipped seven cards on to the pile.

Steve glanced at me sideways. 'One ace.' He put his card down quietly on top of mine.

We all looked at one another. Then we all burst out laugh–ing. I grabbed the bottle and poured another round. I filled Vic's tooth-mug halfway and he patted me on the shoulder. 'I can see you're really getting the hang of this,' he said.

'She's all right.' Steve grunted. 'I told you.'

And I was happy then. For that one moment, anyway. All of a sudden I could see myself actually getting the hang of it, this whole thing, telling the world I had four, seven, fifty-two aces and the world patting me on the shoulder. And me saying 'Fuck off'. All of us keeping a straight face.

*

The next morning was blue. The sun was clear through the bare misshapen branches of the trees. It hurt my eyes. I went to the sink and poured myself a beaker of water. It still had a deposit of sticky crystals in the bottom. A cockroach was lying there on its back, its antennae waving. I tipped it into the sink and washed it down the plughole. I tried to focus my eyes. The crack between the hole and the metal plug was a dark blur.

The heating was on too high, the floor was hot under the soles of my feet. There was nothing I could do to turn it down. I opened my window, the shutters folded back halfway to give just enough light. Then I lay down on the bed, the sun in stripes across the stone floor, our last night's footprints still visible. I picked up a book and tried to read. I remember turning the pages. I remember starting to get interested. Then I heard a slight sound and looked up.

A foot was sticking through my window. A youngish foot in a trainer, greyish and battered. Jeans, a dark flash of sock. I watched it hang in the air, inches from where I lay, then lengthen, feeling for the ground.

I coughed. The foot seemed to shake. Then it pulled back slightly. I stayed quite still, hardly breathing. And it came farther in again. The shoe was waving in the air, the laces were dangling. It was feeling its slow way into my room. Steve? Vic? 'Come in, you fool!' I said loudly. 'Make up your mind! Come in, if you're coming, or go out!'

And the foot withdrew. As if its owner had been burnt. I heard running footsteps. I jumped up from the bed and went to the window to look out, but the back courtyard was already empty. There was only a rack of leaning mopeds, glinting in the sun. Perhaps I'd dreamed it. I shrugged it off. Steve or Vic, playing some trick on me. They played these games all the time.

When they came round that night, I asked them. 'Did you come to see me, earlier?'

They seemed genuinely puzzled. 'No. Why?'

'You didn't come round the back and start to climb in through the window?'

65

'No. Why would we do that?'

'I just wondered.'

'You've been reading too many novels.' I had left my book open, splayed face downwards on the makeshift bedspread. Steve reached out and picked it up. 'What the hell is this?'

'*Le Petit Chose.*'

'*Le Petit* what?'

'*Chose.*'

'Is it any good?'

'I can relate to it.'

'What's it about?'

'Cockroaches,' I said. '*Le cafard*. Teaching.'

'You're too keen, Sarah,' Steve said. 'Give it a rest. Let's play cards.'

'Okay,' I said. 'But no Calvados.'

He got the same dog-eared pack out of his pocket. I found myself looking at his feet. He was wearing trainers, and jeans, and dark socks. It was what we all wore then, we hadn't got the money to buy anything else. 'French Whist?' He cut the pack and held the bottom half out to me. 'What do you fancy? Strip Poker? Or how about Pontoon?'

Francis's house is the house I have visited often in my dreams. The village floats in pale green, the sharp grey spire just emerging from a mist of new leaves. I slow down and take it gently, the little shops and houses with their façades built right against the street, the pavements so narrow you would have to step off them into the roadway to pass someone. A sudden sharp corner that seems to come at me without any warning.

And then I am there. This must be it, this unprepossessing pair of grey cottages joined together by what looks like some kind of shack. It is just as Laurence has described it to me. I lift my fist to the flaking paint of the door and force myself to knock.

And the interior too is just as she has described it – an odd juxtaposition of French *objets d'art* and a residual Englishness that comforts me, in spite of everything. Among these precious lamps and tables, under these expensive facsimiles, there is something else that her account has made no concession to. And his face as he greets me is friendly, without that familiar mask of impersonality, or stress. Alone here with me, he could almost be a different person.

'Sarah. I'm so glad. Come in.'

'You said I should get out here and see you. I did the English thing. I just came.'

'You did the right thing.' He leads me into the main room. It is full of pale green sunlight. Through an open window I can smell the orchard, and the hillside beyond. Somewhere in the distance, a cuckoo. 'Let me just clear this, and we'll have coffee.'

The whole room is a complete mess, the carefully selected furniture half-buried under a drift of books and papers. His leather slippers lie on the rug at an odd angle, as if his feet had just left them. He sweeps sheaves of handwritten notes to one side, into a great pile. He stacks the books one on top of the other, aligning the edges. 'I'm sorry. I was working.'

'Am I disturbing you?'

'Not at all. It's lovely to see you here. I was hoping you'd be brave enough to come. Here, have you read this?' He hands me a book, a fat biography of someone I've never heard of, and leaves me with it in my hands as he goes out to the kitchen. I hear the whir of a coffee-grinder, the bang of a cupboard door. After a few minutes he comes back with two cups of white coffee and a plate of madeleines. 'So. How have you been getting on? Here.' He passes me the plate. 'You need these.'

I take one and sit down. It is mid-morning, the time the emptiness always threatens, even now. 'I've been fine. Coping. I think.'

He is trying not to look at me, my big belly squashed against the edge of the table. I pull my jersey down over the bump. 'It's all under control.'

He is stirring the coffee in his cup. Some of it slops over into the saucer. 'Not all that long to go now.'

'Four weeks. Maybe five.'

'You timed it so well.'

I laugh. It sounds slightly embarrassed. 'I seem to have. Yes.'

He lifts the cup and drinks, the soft shining front hair falling across his eyes. 'And it's all sorted out for next year? The job,

67

and everything? Lervain finally came through?'

'Yes. So it seems.'

'I'm glad. It must be a relief.'

'It is.' There is a long silence, while we drink our coffee. The madeleines are difficult to eat. Crumbs fall from the corners of my mouth into what is left of my lap, and I pick them up one at a time and eat them, hoping he hasn't noticed. The birds outside are singing more loudly than ever.

'More coffee?'

'Please.'

He fetches the coffee-pot, pours, sits down again. Then he leans forward with his elbows on the table. He looks at me intently. 'You had something to ask.'

It's a statement rather than a question. I nod. 'I thought you were the one person I *could* ask . . . the one person kind enough, and honest enough . . . the person who could tell me.'

He is smiling. 'I don't know about kindness. I'll tell you, though. If I can.'

Even so, it's difficult to ask him. 'I . . . You've seen some of my work . . .' I try to begin.

'Yes. They sent what they thought would be a representative sample from England, before you came. Lervain handled it, but several of us got to see it and discuss the candidates. I liked what you were doing. Though I didn't think you were the most obvious choice, actually. It was the Ph.D. that swung it. Lervain loved that.'

I feel a flush rising to my neck, my face. 'What I was thinking . . . What I really wanted to ask you . . .'

His hand across the table uncurls, flattens itself, covered with fine hairs. 'Ask.'

I swallow. Then I say it quickly. 'Do you think I'm good enough? Can I ever be good enough . . . to make a career of this? Is what I do . . . what I am . . . ever going to be . . . acceptable?'

He withdraws his arm and covers his face with his hands. The light in the room is so green it is almost gold. Somewhere, the cuckoo still calls, a long way away, beyond the trees. *No*, I think. I'm not. *No*. He is going to say no.

And then he takes his two hands from his face and looks at me. 'Sarah,' he says, 'are you sure you want to? Is this really going to be what you want? Will it give you what you think it will? Good minds don't necessarily make good scholars. Have you ever thought that perhaps you'll be *bored*?'

The silence between us is thick, almost unbreathable. My voice shakes. 'Thanks.'

'Think about it.'

I start to push back my chair, but the legs catch in a fold of his expensive carpet. For a moment I almost topple. I clutch at the edge of the table with both hands. 'Thank you,' I tell him. 'It wasn't a fair question. Forgive me.' I stand up clumsily, my body heavy and awkward, bumping against the wrought iron standard lamp that is just at my shoulder and making it rock. I put out a hand to steady it.

'Games for grown-ups, Sarah. Are you sure you can handle it?'

'Games for grown-ups? Is that what you play?'

'*Me?* No, I . . .' Francis looks down at his hands. 'Not very well, anyway.'

Suddenly I want to hug him, to reach out and touch him somehow, but I don't dare. 'Francis, thank you,' I say again. I pull the sweater down over the bulge, almost fiercely. 'I won't forget this.'

'You talk as if you're leaving.'

'Perhaps I am leaving. I get the feeling a part of my life is just ending . . . in a way.'

'Lives are always ending.' He is smiling as he sees me to the door. He doesn't kiss me, or shake my hand. 'And beginning.' He only looks down at me, and smiles.

I feel ever more awkward now when I walk into that class. The little room is crowded with desks, with faces, the whole scenario too tight to contain us. And every week now when I walk in they all look at me. Every pair of eyes scans the great lump of my belly, and quickly looks away, hands fiddling with pencils or the catches of briefcases, faces studiously avoiding me, pretending to be preoccupied with something scrawled on the top sheet of a wad of notes, or a half-used bus ticket found on the floor. And Marthe has withdrawn into herself now. She sits at the back of the class, hunched into her shapeless clothes, a visible ghost. Sometimes she lifts her head and leans forward across the desk, her chin in her hands, glaring at me with something that looks like hatred. Once she is so cramped and dejected that I look at her as I ask a question, willing her to glance up. 'Marthe?' I say. And when she raises her head I see her expression go suddenly bland and flat, and I realise that she has been laughing.

I am panicked now by that class, because she is in it. Each Friday afternoon when I walk in they seem to be watching me that much more closely. And Marthe herself is ever quieter, exuding a kind of mute hostility. Each week I am that much less in control, that much more forgetful. One week I come without my notes.

It is not just my notes, either. It is the grammar book with the exercises I have been told to use with them each week. It is the word-games I have devised for them, based on their own most current errors. It is the sheaf of translations, with their marks.

For a moment I almost forget where I am. My head has no words long enough for this, in any language. I am English. They are French. And I have a whole short lifetime of vocabulary, idioms, usage, contexts to offer them, in myself. But *two hours*? My whole life wouldn't fill two hours. Perhaps twenty minutes. And then what would I do? Escape through the nearest door, to discover it was only a broom-cupboard? Hide there in the dark among the mops and dusters until the two hours were finally up and I could hear them all starting to pack up and leave? 'I'm so sorry,' I say to them. 'I've forgotten to bring all my stuff.'

They smile. Then Jean-Luc says quickly, 'There's no class in here after this one. How long will it take you to drive back and get your things?'

'An hour, at least.'

'It doesn't matter. You can make up the time at the end. We'll all wait. Such great ignorance isn't going to go away!'

The others all nod. I can't believe it. But I lumber downstairs and out to where my car is parked at the back of the building. I drive back to the cottage as fast as I can. The journey seems twice as long as usual. At one stage I get stuck behind a dustcart and trail it through a village, cursing. My file is on the kitchen table, where I left it.

It has taken me an hour and twenty-three minutes. I burst into the classroom, my face bright red, my lower back throb–bing. The file of work is in my hand. Jean-Luc stops talking to the girl next to him and sits up straight. He smiles at me. They all smile. 'You see?' he says in English. 'We waited. You are worth waiting for.'

I pull back the black elastic and open the file on my desk. I hand them their marked exercises. One by one they lean back in their chairs, screwing up their eyes to decipher my English handwriting. But when I come to Marthe's I see she has gone.

There are only days to go now before the baby is due. 'D-Day,' my childbirth manual insists on calling it. I try not to admit to myself how frightened I am.

But the dreams give me away – dark dreams full of epi–durals and shots of pethidine, legs parted on emptiness, black rubber masks hissing gas and air. Dreams of strange children that spring from my womb already articulate, able to talk in long multilingual sentences, five-year-olds that reach out to me and hold my hand. Once, a luminous dream about my own mother, my own birth, from which I awake in a state of sexual arousal, for no obvious reason. Never have I dreamed so vividly. And the whole magic-lantern-show criss-crossed by words. Your words. *'Moi, je suis charpentier.'* And then, *'Nous ferons ce que nous pourrons pour vous aider.'* Words rushing through darkness like trains, or cars, like a battered Minivan cutting its slow zigzag of light through the Pyrenees, or like a plane, a small winking planet above Paris, on its way west.

> *Près de nous Jésus grandira*
> *Et bientôt il vous aidera,*
> *Et la sagesse il apprendra.*

And I wake up wondering about the baby, about what language I shall use to speak to her in, what language she will use to communicate with me. And about wisdom. About the points of contact between wisdom and kindness.

A couple of weeks before the baby is due I visit the restored cathedral again. Do you remember it, how we went in there that first sunny morning and wandered around, looking at the old photographs mounted on those screens? How we talked about what it must have been like, before the Allies almost levelled it to a heap of smoking rubble? The locals coming up out of the cellars they'd been hiding in and trying to make the best of the shell that was left? How we went out then into the sunshine and saw the market with its flapping awnings? And bought artichokes and plums?

And today I visit it again. The photographs are still there, just as they were, only slightly faded or yellow in places where the light from one of the high windows has struck them too directly. Only the odd drawing-pin missing.

And I stand and rock back on my heels and look at them a second time, my hands clasped over the smock, the child moving under my skin. An old man in a cap picks his way over the stones, his face gaunt and unshaven, his eyes in shadow. I feel a small area of pressure just under my ribs, pushing outwards – the sole of a small foot. I push down on it with my hand and it moves away, kicks out in another direction. In one shot a woman with a hat stands holding the hands of her two children. Her tweed coat has an astrakhan collar. The little girls look serious, staring wide-eyed into the camera against a background of smoke.

The door of the departmental staffroom isn't locked. I push it open. As I stand there in the doorway they both look up.

I catch the slightest trace of irritation as it passes across Lervain's face. Then it is gone, and the expression is only one of enquiry. Laurence looks blank, as if she has been concentrating, as if she has been dreaming and is only half awake. 'Excuse me. I didn't mean to interrupt.' I tread past them, towards the back table under the window, where my piles of photocopies wait.

Lervain nods. Then he goes back to the manuscript pages in front of him. He points to a word with the nib of his pen, circles something on the paper, looks at Laurence. 'This could go, no? You can find some better way to say this, something less heavy and convoluted.'

'Perhaps. Yes.'

'It's an interesting and attractive idea. You just have to frame it more simply.'

'Yes.' She pushes the cloth of her cuffs higher, exposing her thin wrists. Her watch seems to hang loose on the bone. 'This is so helpful.' I feel her voice shake.

I pick up a sheaf of copies and make for the door as quietly as I can. The door-handle gives a loud click.

'Oh, Sarah . . .'

'Yes?' I stand there, frozen, wrong-footed. The door swings to again under my weight.

'I was wondering how you would feel about doing the Charnay dictation this year.'

'I'm sorry?'

'Charnay. We do it every year. Hasn't anyone mentioned it to you? The department always sends someone.'

'Yes?'

'You don't have to do anything. Just go there, just be there for the exam, in case of some technical hitch. People usually enjoy it. An opportunity to mingle inconspicuously with the future military genius of France.' He looks at my shape in the doorway, and gives a short laugh. 'If you wouldn't find it too much, that is, at the moment. If you don't feel like doing it I can ask someone else. But we always try to send the best person we have.'

'Thank you.' I clutch the photocopies to the front of my jersey.

'So you're happy to do it?'

'Of course.'

'You stay overnight with one of the English teachers. He's a charming man. And I believe they pay quite generously. You can drive there in that little orange car of yours. Take your time. See a bit of the countryside.'

'Actually, I'm not driving much these days. Not long journeys, anyway.'

'Is that right?'

'I don't feel very comfortable.' Hannah so close to the wheel, her soft flesh almost unprotected, and the steering column so rigid it could go straight through her. 'I don't think I feel quite safe,' I say to him.

'There's always the train. The train's fairly convenient.'

'Yes. Thank you,' I say again.

'Check in the office about the dates.'

73

'Right.'

Laurence has got up and walked to the window. Lervain's hand lies across the back of the chair where she has just been sitting. Now she stands looking out, turned away from us both. For a split second my eyes slip out of focus and the image is thinned to a bright stick, the sun exploding in her hair.

Last thing I go out to put a bag of rubbish in the dustbin. It has been raining. The night is full of the smell of leaves, dominating the usual reek of silage. As I lift the lid a pool of water that has gathered in the centre spills sideways on to my foot, glistening. The clouds are parting now.

I hear a noise from Dominique's kitchen and she comes out, staggering towards me across the gravel with something awkward and heavy in her arms. I hold the lid for her while she puts her rubbish in on top of mine. Then I replace it.

'It's clearing,' she says to me. 'A fine day tomorrow, apparently.'

'Good.'

'How are you?'

I try to make out her face in the darkness, but there is only the pale glint of her eyes. And I am invisible too, swallowed by the black air of the birches and sycamores that grow here. We are only eyes to each other, and voices. 'I'm fine,' I say. 'Thanks.'

'Sure?'

'I think so.'

'Well . . .' She shifts her feet and the gravel crunches. 'You know where I am. If anything happens . . . At any time . . . We're there, with the phone. The middle of the night, whatever. Don't worry about waking us.'

'Thank you. You're very kind.'

'*No!*' She makes an odd, gruff noise, almost like clearing her throat. 'It's not kindness! It's called survival.' My eyes are getting used to the darkness now. I can almost see her face. 'Survival . . . and having been through it myself, when I was your age. It's all quite natural. You mustn't be frightened. There's nothing to be frightened of. Having a baby isn't something you can do well, or badly. You'll be fine. The baby'll

74

be fine. They won't have to choose between you. Stories, all that.'

'The books make it sound as if there's a right way to do it. And by extension, a way of failing.'

'Rubbish. You shouldn't read them.'

'I know. But I can't help it.'

'Relax.' I can just see her lower her face to try and make out mine. 'Silly girl.'

'I'll try.' I turn to go. I take a few steps away from her, towards my own doorway.

But she calls out to me, 'Oh, Sarah . . .' She pronounces it in the French way. Sarah Bernhardt or a character in a novel of the 1920s.

I stop. I turn back. 'Yes?'

'Have you seen the comet?'

'The what?'

'The comet. It's the last night, they said. And the others have all been cloudy.'

'Is it visible?'

She comes over to me and puts her hands on my shoulders. She turns me almost due north, towards the sharp end of the plough. 'Look.'

And there it is, just over the trees, resembling any star, except that it is ringed by a whitish blur. Beautiful, and disappointing. 'It's a small moon,' I say.

'The halo?'

I shiver. I'm suddenly conscious of the wet in my shoe. 'Bad weather?'

'Rubbish.' She puts her arm round my shoulders and gives me a sudden quick hug. Then she lets me go. 'Just weather. Real weather.' It is so quiet as we stand there. I can hear the drops from the trees. '*Un ange passe,*' she says. Then, 'Relax. Don't worry. Don't read too much. A month from now it'll all be over.'

Slowly the city slides away from me, through dirty windows. The greyish-white apartment-blocks with their uniform balconies, shuttered streets, the occasional greening vein of trees. Then the depots, the industrial buildings, gathering speed as they slip past me to become a part of what I have left behind, faster and faster. And finally the open spaces, the woods, sloping fields and cows. And at their edges the mist of new leaves just beginning.

At Rouviers I have to wait an hour between trains. I go into the little station café and sit down with a big breakfast *café au lait*. The small room is quite crowded already. I look up and see a young couple shepherding their two small children in my direction.

The man sits next to me, the woman on the plastic bench opposite, with the two little boys. Within minutes the kids' mouths are orange with grenadine.

'I told you it would have been better to do this Tuesday.' He lifts the wedge-shaped water-jug and pours water into his glass. As if by magic, the clear liquid goes milky. 'Didn't I tell you?'

One of the little boys twists in his seat to look at her. 'When do we get there? *Dis, maman*. Can we climb right up to the top?'

She seems to ignore him, as if she hasn't heard. As if she hardly knows who he is. She sits gazing out towards the platform, as if she is quite unaware of his presence. Then she leans forwards slightly and strokes the little boy's head, combing his silky dark hair with her fingers.

'I told you today was a bad idea,' the man says. She lifts her face and looks at him. He raises his glass and takes a big mouthful. 'Tuesday would have been a lot better. We wouldn't have had all these crowds, Tuesday.'

'I was working on Tuesday. You know I always work Tuesdays.'

'You could have changed your day for once.'

'He doesn't like it when I do. It complicates everything.'

'That's his problem.'

Her voice suddenly has an edge to it. 'Why should he like it? He pays me to be dependable. Is that so hard for you to grasp? And anyway, with the boys . . .'

He lifts his glass again, almost drains it in one go. He puts it down on the table just slightly too hard. I feel the table shake. He wipes his mouth on his sleeve, scowling at her. The scowl extends to include the whole group, me, the little boys even. He grunts. 'I told you Tuesday would have been better. The

76

trains wouldn't have been held up. We'd've missed all these crowds, if we'd done it Tuesday.'

But she is not looking at him. Her head is bent as she reaches down into her bag for a box of Kleenex. She pulls out a tissue and wets it with a few drops of water from the jug. Gently she starts to wipe the red-orange stains from the little boys' upturned faces.

The little train that is to take me to Charnay is quite different. I have left the crowds behind. I am almost alone in the first carriage. I sit right at the front. Next to me the driver sits hidden behind his partition, working his invisible controls. The single track stretches away in front of me, the metal wheels under me slowly digesting the kilometres, the twin rails converging into nothing.

The sun is stronger now, piercing the network of branches hazed with green, the banks mottled white, gold, mauve with clumps of wild flowers, the colours merging in a haze of running brush-strokes. Sun pours in through the glass, warming my body. And the baby seems to sense it and starts to move again.

Kicks. Slow-motion somersaults. Punches. A kind of tactile laughter under my skin, a gymnastic of future possibility. Training for a life. Training for breath, food, for the crying that is our first language, our only common tongue.

Hannah. The tight fist of limbs that will become Hannah. In front of us both, the narrow rails unwind, smoothing the contours of the local geography, bridging valleys with embankments, cutting through hillsides, curving sweetly round the fringes of a copse. She and I, riding the track together towards our eventual destination, the point where the rails converge. The two of us increasingly heavy and hot and tired, travelling towards our welcome party of young soldiers, their pens poised, their faces attentive, their close-cropped heads raised to listen.

I pick out M. Lambert immediately from the small cluster of people waiting at the barrier. He is the one in the white turtleneck and English-looking tweed jacket. He smiles at me, friendly, then suddenly embarrassed. He stretches out his right hand.

77

Together we drive through the narrow cobbled streets of the town to his house just outside the old walls. A ruined fragment is still half-visible from the landing window, its cracks sprouting small ferns. He shows me up to a room under the eaves. The window is open on to other roofs, the light curtain blowing. It is almost English. He puts my overnight bag down at the foot of the bed. 'Well, this is it.' He is trying not to let his eyes look any lower than my shoulders. 'I hope you'll be comfortable. It's a pleasure to have you here. I expect you'd like a few moments to yourself to unpack, put yourself in some sort of order. Claire and I will be just downstairs, if you should need anything.' Finally he has lost the battle: his eyes move across me, and then quickly past me, to the window. 'Or perhaps you could do with a rest?' I turn my head and look where he is looking. Just outside the window a lilac branch waves, the head of bloom still in bud, a cone of tight small green spheres that in a week or two will have turned into so many white stars.

I must have slept. Through my eyelashes it is dusk already. I sit up on the bed and swing my feet to the floor. The spearhead of lilac is almost black now, against the greenish curve of the sky. I flex my fingers. I move my bare toes on the rug. My ankles aren't as swollen as they were.

I change my crumpled dress for another one I have in my bag. I brush my hair. I would like to clean my teeth, but I'm not sure where the bathroom is. I rub the crumbs of sleep from the corners of my eyes.

The house is quite quiet. Only the noise of wood-pigeons in the trees outside and the faint omnipresent hum of the town. Then gradually my ears begin to pick up the soft exchange of voices somewhere underneath me. M. Lambert's low growl, and an answering murmur. I tiptoe to the head of the stairs and stand listening for a moment, but still I can't make out the words. The French intonation rises and rises under me in a series of unanswered questions.

Softly I go down. They are in the kitchen together, their backs towards me as I stand in the doorway. He is drying the morning's breakfast dishes, a tea-towel in his hand, an apron knotted at his waist. She seems to be slicing something into a

78

pastry case, the point of her right elbow jerking rhythmically to the crisp hiss of the knife.

They turn and face me. They smile. She bends to the fridge and takes out a big jug of something. 'Hello. Welcome.' She fills a tumbler and puts it in my hand.

It is fruit-juice, a mixture of something I can't quite place. Lime and passion-fruit? Grapefruit? Pineapple? 'You poor thing. You must be tired out,' she says.

'May I help you . . . do something?' I gesture at the para- phernalia of cooking strewn across the formica table.

'No. No. You just sit here for a while and relax. There's nothing to do, really.' She waves her arm towards the seating area in the main room, a comfortable arrangement of low leather chairs.

Everywhere there are books – on the floor, on the coffee- table. A little gleaming knife for the uncut pages. And along two walls of the room, from floor to ceiling, big rough book- cases crammed with stuff – the austere white spines of new French fiction, plays, poetry, philosophy. Pléiade editions still in their grey cardboard boxes, the ribbon bookmarks pro- truding like the tongues of small snakes. An orange rank of Penguins, streaked here and there with a band of some other colour. Golding, Hemingway, Isherwood. Colette, Duras, Faulkner. Yourcenar, Zola. My eyes follow the line of names, half hypnotised by this arrangement for two voices. 'You both read a lot,' I say. I take a sip from my glass and gulp it awkwardly. Even before I swallow, I know I am going to choke.

I suppress it, though. Mind over matter. My eyes are water- ing furiously. I force myself to put down the glass slowly and raise my hand to my face to brush the tears discreetly away. I don't think either of them has noticed that I am having a hard time breathing. My throat aches with the effort not to cough. For a couple of minutes I can't speak.

After dinner we sit back in the same chairs, over cups of decaffeinated coffee. 'You'll find it's all very simple,' M. Lambert says.

'That's what M. Lervain told me.'

'If we leave here about seven tomorrow morning, we can

be at the school by half-past and I'll have time to show you the room, before the pupils arrive.'

'What time does the exam start?'

'Eight-fifteen.'

'And I don't actually have to do anything? Just be there?'

'That's it. You're just a back-up, a fall-back procedure. Just in case there should be some accident. Fire or flood. Earthquake. In case they should have sent the wrong tape. Or in case there's a power-cut. And even then . . .'

'You could run it on a battery machine.'

'Exactly.'

'So really, I'm completely supernumerary.'

He laughs, kindly. 'But the regulations say we have to have someone. And it's a pleasure for us, to meet you and have you to stay here in our home with us. Though in the eighteen years I've been doing this, nothing has ever gone wrong once. All that linguistic authenticity . . .' he looks at me and smiles again, with his eyes, 'has lain fallow, so to speak.'

'Yes.' I lift the tiny china cup and take a careful sip. I don't choke this time. 'Tell me about your pupils. Are they . . . soldierly?'

He laughs outright then, and his wife with him, the two of them together. But still it isn't unkind. 'Not very. Not yet. They're wonderfully well brought up. The cream of France.'

'They're very normal, though, Jean-Yves. Don't give her the wrong impression. They do all the usual teenage things, I'm sure.'

He lays his hands flat on the cloth of his thighs, palm downwards, and spreads his fingers. Raises his fingers slightly. Lowers them again. He is still smiling. 'Claire's right, of course. They're not saints. But they do have a certain . . . sense of responsibility. A certain seriousness, a rare understanding of country and cultural identity. Or at least, that's what we try to give them.'

'And an understanding of others,' Claire puts in. 'The school particularly insists on the ethical perspective.'

I'm lost for words. 'And do they . . .?' I say. 'What do you actually . . . ?'

He jumps up from his chair and goes to a corner of the bookcase, where fat files are stacked vertically, so tightly wedged that he curses as he tries to extract one, and sucks at a fingernail. Then he is beside me on the leather sofa, the heavy folder open on his knee. He flips through the pages. 'Here. You see . . . This is the kind of thing I've been doing with them lately. I've built up quite a library of texts over the years.'

I follow his pointing finger across the titles. *Hamlet*, 'Ode to a Grecian Urn', *Silas Marner, Murder in the Cathedral, Krapp's Last Tape*. The breadth and scope are astonishing. 'But this is like a university level course,' I say, 'in taster form.'

He looks at me shyly, gratified. 'Do you think so?'

I hesitate for a moment. 'And you don't do anything . . . with a . . . specifically military focus?'

He frowns. 'Why should I? It's not about death, being a good soldier. Its about what's worth defending. It's about the living.'

'Jean-Yves . . .' Claire stands up, reaching for our empty cups.

'Do you think they're . . . *short-changed*?' He says it in English. With his brush haircut and earnestness he is almost like a pupil himself.

The folder is still spread across the sofa cushion beside me. *To be or not to be* . . . I close my eyes for a moment. Then I open them. 'Not at all.' His face is out of focus, separating, a horizontal blur of faces, all equally earnest, all topped by the same bristling hair. 'I think they're very lucky,' I tell him.

Outside it is surprisingly cold. The grass at the edges of the gravel paths is still wet. Our feet crunch as we circle the equestrian statue, the horse's flanks streaked green under the spurs, the rider's face encrusted. In the arched stone doorway we stop. We make an incongruous couple. And behind us that world of dripping trees. When we enter the exam room I am shivering.

A high moulded ceiling arches over us, the central chandelier astonishingly ugly in its complicated star of plaster, the relief blurred with age, the symmetrical pattern of indentations half-flattened under coat after coat of matt paint. White, or pale grey. It is hard to tell. The rows of empty desks stretch away from us, right to the back of the room, all facing front, each with its sheet of blank paper, each with its number. No

81

graffiti, no obscene drawings gouged in them with a knife-blade or the point of a compass, no girls' names. Just inkwells set in smooth wood. M. Lambert puts down a small sealed package. He glances at his wristwatch, then at the heavy old clock on the wall above us. 'Well, anyway,' he says to me, 'we can try out the machine.'

'Right.' My voice is high, nervous, shaking absurdly. My teeth are starting to chatter.

He turns to look at me. 'Are you cold?'

'Not really.'

'Here.' He pulls out a chair. 'Do sit down. I'll just play around with a few switches.'

He bends over the tape-recorder. Outside the sun is starting to come through, a few pale shafts piercing the grey. The child inside me gives a sudden lurch.

I hear a button click, the sound of a tape being loaded. Then, booming, gigantic, the voice of Brassens:

> 'Non, ce n'était pas le Radeau
> De la Méduse, ce bateau . . .'

I jump. But almost immediately the voice shrinks to human proportions. 'Sorry.'

'It's all right.'

'I didn't mean to do that.'

Around us, in the deserted aisles, in the four high corners of the room, the voice comes and goes – louder, softer, louder again, darker, lighter, clearer. M. Lambert turns to look at me. 'Does that sound about right to you?'

I can make out every word. 'It sounds fine.'

'We can't try it with the real thing, unfortunately. We're not allowed to open the package until the very last moment, in front of them all.'

'Of course.' I take a deep breath, as deep as I can with the baby's feet pressing up under my rib-cage, compressing the space that ought to belong to my lungs. I bite back a sour belch of half-digested bread and coffee. I turn my face to the window.

'Don't worry.'

But before I can answer him the boys have begun to file in. Not loudly. There is no talking. Only the occasional small crash as someone bangs into a desk or steps backwards in confusion, looking for his number. A mischievous exchange of glances near the door. In the second aisle someone stoops to tie a shoelace and the kids behind him almost plough into his bent back. Then they are all seated, some staring out of the window, some down at the blank sheets, some looking at M. Lambert, twirling their pens between their fingers or tapping their feet. One or two openly curious, staring at me. I put my hands in my pockets and shrug the two sides of my jacket closer, until they almost meet. No one has told me whether I am allowed to smile. Above us the second hand of the clock jerks forwards. '*Bon*,' M. Lambert says.

They all look up as he tears open the package. He unfolds a sheet of printed paper and hands it to me. I watch as he tightens the tape on the spool, loads it, straightens up. From his own sheet of instructions he reads something, loudly and clearly. '*Chaque phrase, ou morceau de phrase, vous sera lue deux fois . . .*' The lines of faces are suddenly fused in a single anxiety, the tense delicate dark features and the tense smooth fair features the same. Something at the back of the eyes. Pens at the ready. The button clicks.

And a voice rises – slows to a growl – trips into a female register, incomprehensible. For a moment they look at one another, wondering if this is English, if this is how a foreign language is meant to sound. The voice chatters its monkey-gibberish and then sinks again, a very old man's dying gasp. There is a last hiccup. Then they start to laugh.

M. Lambert quiets them with a restraining gesture of his hand. '*Allez, ça suffit. Ce n'est pas grave.* It seems we shall have to avail ourselves of the services of . . .' He turns to me.

The paper is shaking between my fingers so that I can hardly see it. The words are vibrating in front of my eyes. I stand up, swaying slightly, supporting my right elbow with my left hand. The breath-groups are neatly marked with oblique strokes. ' "I rowed in the dark",' I begin. ' "I rowed in the dark".' I wait for a few seconds, until the first few pairs of eyes look up at me, the pens lifted over the page. ' ". . . keeping the wind in my face." '

It is almost too much. Fifty pairs of eyes fixed on my body, my puffy cheeks, my ankles, my gaping jacket. Fifty pairs of

83

young eyes, their whites almost impossibly clear. Fifty darkening pages. Fifty pens scratching across from left to right, the half-formed handwriting of so many children, panic-stricken or unconcerned. Splattered with blots. And my own voice leading them, in a language they can barely understand. Transparent as it is. ' "I pulled it along in the dark water." ' The breath-control is getting even harder now. At the oblique strokes I am half-gasping. But I have come almost to the end. I am nearing the bottom. ' "I pulled it along in the dark water." '

And almost on cue the fifty pairs of eyes look up at me. The fifty pens are finally capped. And the room around me begins to spin, the child a hard indigestible knot against my solar plexus, my legs crumpling under me like two pieces of rotten wood.

'Are you sure you're all right now?' Claire is driving me through the jumbled streets, towards the little station. We pass a public garden, with its cluster of swings, its gravel walks, an ornamental basin with a small fountain playing. An old church. I turn round briefly to check my overnight bag is still in the back. The effort of twisting in my seat makes me feel slightly sick.

'I'm fine. Honestly.'

'You gave them all quite a surprise this morning.'

'I gave myself quite a surprise. Not to mention . . .'

'But you're okay?'

I can feel the baby moving in my belly, a sleepy aftershock, like acquiescence. 'I'm fine. We're both fine.' I look at her and smile.

She is concentrating on the road. Almost in front of us an old lady steps out, a wheeled shopping-basket dragged at her heels, on her way to market. Claire brakes and swerves, hits the centre of the steering-wheel with her hand. The old lady looks up. For perhaps half a mile the blank features stay with me, the old eyes in their pouches of loose wrinkles, uncomprehending. We turn into the small oval turning-area in front of the station building and come to a halt.

Before I can even find the clasp of my seat-belt she is out of the car and opening the door on my side. 'No rush. We're in good time. Let me help you with your bag.'

'No, really. I . . .'

But she reaches determinedly into the back of the car and pulls it out. 'I'm going to stay with you until the train arrives. We wouldn't want you keeling over again, among strangers!'

'You're very kind.'

'Don't be silly.'

She locks the car behind us and follows me into the shadowy ticket hall, then out on to the platform. The skin at the corners of her eyes looks tight and tired, as if she hasn't slept. She sighs as she puts the bag down at our feet.

We walk up the platform slowly, almost to the end. I follow the four bright rails with my eyes, to where they merge into a single track and finally disappear into the base of a curving mass of trees.

I look at my watch. Ten minutes to wait, still. I search my imagination for something I can say to her.

But she is the one to speak first. 'I hope it all goes well.'

For a moment I am puzzled. Then I see her looking. 'Oh.' I hunch my shoulders, so that the shape of my body is less visible. 'Oh. Yes. I'm sure it will.'

'You know . . .' She turns her head away from me for a moment with what must be embarrassment. Then she looks back. 'Jean-Yves and I . . .'

I wait. She is still holding the long shoulder-strap of my bag, smoothing and kneading it between her fingers. 'We're not going to have any children. Ever.'

'Oh?' I want to sit down, but the benches are a whole trek away, under the overhang. I shift my weight from one leg to the other. I say carefully, 'Well, I think people often manage to lead more complete and satisfying lives if they don't.'

She bites her lip. Then she says, simply, 'It isn't by choice.'

'I see.' Our two shadows stretch away from us obliquely towards the edge of the platform, mine thicker, undulating slightly over a bump, hers stick-thin. At the edge both of us are cut off, ending suddenly just below the shoulder in a straight line. 'I'm sorry.'

'Don't be sorry. As you say, our lives are very full. And we have each other.'

The trees that run along the edge of the opposite platform are suddenly a blur, their knobbed outlines melting and twisting, the little flags of first leaves disappearing into a greenish glaze on mutilated limbs. I blink, and the green-gold pennants reappear. 'And you're happy,' I say to her. 'I could feel it.'

She smooths the black strap under her fingers. A floating corner of silk scarf lifts against her face, and she sneezes. She gets out a handkerchief and blows her nose. When she has put it back in her pocket, she says, 'And you, you're . . . alone?'

'Yes.'

'For how long?'

'Since October.'

We both stare into the distance, towards the small nick in the landscape where the train will appear. Nothing yet. 'He was American,' I say suddenly. 'He was called Joseph. He went home in October.'

Her eyes meet mine. 'Was he obliged to go?'

There is a long silence. Somewhere far away from us, inside the station building, a bell rings. 'I suppose he was, in a way.'

Now at last there is something, a small dark plug that grows almost imperceptibly larger as we watch, filling the gap of sky between trees and far embankment and still growing – a toy – a child's ride – a train. I hear myself say: 'He wouldn't have wanted to be here. He wasn't interested in babies. We weren't together for very long – only a matter of months, really. But it was long enough for me to know that about him. He didn't want kids. He didn't want . . . commitment.' I make a face as I say the word. 'He really wouldn't want to be here with me.'

She has to shout now, to make herself heard. 'And what about you? Would you want him? Don't you need him at all?'

'Oh, me . . .' She is playing with the strap of my bag again. I take it gently from between her fingers and hoist the dead weight on to my shoulder. 'Not under those conditions, no. Under those conditions I don't think I ought to need anyone.'

The train screeches to a halt in front of us, the heads of our two shadows swallowed under the wheels. Near us a door crashes open. I move towards it, the bag banging awkwardly against my thigh. Someone leans out and takes it from me, lifts it into the train, extends a hand to help me in after it. But before I can get in she has stepped forward, grasping my two hands. Are there tears in her eyes? 'Well,' she says. 'Whatever the conditions, if you do decide to let yourself need someone, you know where we are.'

I get into the train and sit down. It is more crowded than when I came, and the seat I find is facing backwards. As the train moves off I see Claire's solitary figure on the platform, not smiling or waving, shrinking as the distance between us grows. When we clatter over the points on to the single track, she still hasn't turned away.

In this direction the journey is not so easy. I have to re-imagine the city, prepare myself again by visualising their faces one by one. Marthe, Laurence, Lervain, Francis – I turn them in my mind like coins. Heads or tails. As I strain to recreate them the stamped features escape me, blurring under my thumb, rubbed away like old kings and queens with too much use. I'm so tired. On the other side of the window a sudden embankment throws us into near-darkness. My face looks back at me, half-transparent, the running contours of the bank streaking it with shadow, the branches whipping across it, provoking no reaction. The baby is asleep now. Inside me I can feel nothing. The other passengers seem scarcely to notice me, or register that I am pregnant. Their eyes pass over me, impersonal, indifferent, the eyes of people I have already left behind.

The station café is not the same now, either. Oddly, in spite of the crowded train, it is almost empty. This time I have only twenty-five minutes to wait.

But I buy myself another cup of coffee from the same woman behind the counter. I sit at the same table. This time the places across from me are unoccupied.

When the train comes in it takes me by surprise. Somehow I get myself out on to the platform and into the nearest compartment. An elderly man is sitting by the glass, facing an elderly woman who must be his wife. I push between them and sink into the nearest seat.

Little by little the people on the platform thin out, threading their way towards the exit. One or two still stand a few feet back, smiling sheepishly at someone in the train. Somewhere to the rear, a door slams. Then I remember my bag.

87

Christ I have left it in the station café, under the table where I was sitting. *'Pardon. Excusez-moi.'* I almost fall against the old woman's knees. I force my way out, half-stumbling as my feet hit the platform, running clumsily across the concrete, crashing the café door back against the wall.

It is there. Under the table, where I left it. I yank on the strap and the bag slides towards me, snagging only briefly on the table's metal legs. I haven't even got time to hoist it on to my shoulder. I clutch it to my chest, a huge black bundle I can hardly see over. In the doorway I almost collide with a workman in blue overalls. Beyond him, next to the platform, the train is waiting, the people inside frozen in their separate poses of departure. On the platform itself a young man stands with his right hand half-raised.

But I make it. I just make it. Somehow I reach the nearest door and almost fall in. Somehow I sink down in the same empty seat, still holding my bag tightly on my lap.

I am sweating. My body is telling me something, its own wisdom of heart and lungs and thirst. My scalp prickles with sweat; the clothes are plastered to the small of my back like a poultice. The blood thumps in my ears, louder than any other noise, throbbing in a vein at the side of my neck. My whole body is a single pulse, the child momentarily drowned out, nonexistent. I can no longer even feel her, no longer recognise her soft flutters and lurches, the weird rhythms of her unvolitional purpose. I am going back, back to them all, back to all the old places. In a month or two I shall be able to call my body my own.

And it's as if the place I'm really going back to is you – that tiny flat where we lived together, its check muslin curtains threaded on wire at the glass door, its dented aluminium saucepans. The diurnal cacophony of mopeds on the other side of the wall.

The door will be unlocked. I shan't even need to break and enter. I shall sit on my low chair and look out over that scrubby tree in the yard. And I shall tell the whole thing, from start to finish. Not to you – you'll be gone already, or at least preoccupied, your mind focused on the urgent business of leaving. But to the place itself. To the check curtains, the saucepans, the passing strangers. To the fireplace masked with tissue paper that rattled in the wind at night, filling our sleep with flames and fissures, dreams of disaster that would make us laugh when we remembered them at breakfast. To the mantelpiece festooned with congealed drips in nine colours of wax.

I am walking along the rue des Vergers. Spring sweaters are tastefully arranged in windows, the knitted cotton folds pulled into seductive shapes, a scarf flowing at a neckline, echoing an understated shade of blue. Skirts of impeccable cut that deny any suggestion that they might one day be inhabited by flesh. A discreet necklace. And my own reflection, drowning in glass.

A *parfumerie*, its matching bottles aligned in descending rank. An advertisement for some weight-reducing cream, *contre la cellulite*. And in there, on the other side of the expensive display, I catch sight of Laurence.

She has her back towards me, her long fair hair tied back with a dark roll of silk, her head bent. She is choosing something. I see her reach into her purse and extract the notes. I see her put the little ribboned package in her shoulder-bag. I wait for her in the doorway, the white cardboard thigh of the advertisement stretching its perfectly matt, undimpled surface under the cardboard hand.

She comes towards me, closing her bag. She looks up. She stops in her tracks. 'Sarah.'

'Laurence. Hello.'

'When did you get back?'

'Yesterday.'

She swings the strap up on to her shoulder in one graceful movement. She pushes an escaping wisp of hair from her face. 'How was it?'

'Fine. It was an experience.' The breeze is picking at the little strand of hair again, blowing it across her eyes. 'I enjoyed it. Well . . . most of it. How are you?'

'Oh . . .' She pouts. 'It goes on. As usual. Lervain . . .' She stops, biting the tip of her finger.

'Have you seen him?'

'Oh. Well. Not really.' She is on edge, still fidgeting with things – her collar, a loose piece of cotton at the eye of a button. 'Look, Sarah, I'm sorry . . .'

'What's the matter?' My voice sounds so English.

'I'm just seeing someone, to sort something out. I can't stay and talk. I'm sorry.'

' "Sort something out"?' The expression strikes me oddly.

She opens her bag again and pulls out a handkerchief. She blows her nose. 'Well, not sort out, exactly.'

And suddenly I know. The cardboard woman seems to be rocking to and fro on her plastic mount. The little bottles could contain anything – neat alcohol, poison. The child in me has gone quite still. It might be dead.

She puts her long hand on my arm. 'Don't worry. It was all very informal. Nothing was actually decided.'

'But it will be, soon.'

'Well . . . It's nearly the end of the year. He has to decide before too long.'

I can see them all, the faces arranged round the huge shiny meeting-room table, in descending order. Lervain, Paul, Francis, Mireille . . . Laurence not among them. She is somewhere else, pacing a closed room. And almost immediately she is here in the rue des Vergers, wondering which perfume to buy. Yves Saint Laurent? Or something even more sophisticated? Suddenly I seem to catch the smell of those child-soldiers, in their unbroken lines. 'Well,' I say. 'Congratulations. To you both. He certainly picked his moment. Just when he knew I'd be away. He's a fine strategist. Someone ought to promote him to something higher up. He's wasted here.'

'Sarah . . .'

And the words of the dictation come back to me. *I did not feather the oars because the wind was with us. I knew my hands would blister and I wanted to delay it as long as I could.* I can see it in memory, the breath-groups indicated by neat diagonal lines. Hear my own voice repeating them endlessly, practising after the event, just in case the current should stop flowing, in case rain should get in and cause a short in the wiring, in case the equipment should suddenly break down.

4

THESE DAYS I MISS YOU almost impossibly. The shape of your long square fingers round a pen or a cup, the neat oval of your skull through your dark hair. Your mouth. Your foreign soft voice somewhere behind me, breathing into my neck.

We were happy, surely, at first? We used to laugh enough as we cooked together in the evening. We would forget the wine in our glasses as we talked. Next morning we would discover them, the dregs in each thick base dried to a purple crust.

And in those long afternoons when neither of us had any teaching we would go to bed. We would get up when the first mopeds started to buzz past, on their way home. It seems to me I can still hear them, those mopeds. Even from here. Even from this stone cottage in the middle of nowhere, where the only familiar sounds belong to birds or cows, or to the milk truck revving on the steep slope of the lane.

Now it is winter. Five-thirty, and we are already in darkness. But you still have hours of daylight in front of you. Where you are, hardly anyone is thinking of going to bed.

I am almost always cold. Even with the upstairs heater going full blast, the bedroom is never really warm. The bed stretches its expanse of icy white sheet, and my body can never quite fill it, the heat of my one skin never quite reaches the corners. If I feel outwards with my toes or fingers I can still sense the cold coming. Every morning I wake curled in on myself in a tight ball, defending myself against the encroaching chill.

Downstairs, I feed logs to the woodstove. Robert is kind. He keeps my stock of wood replenished and I have only to trudge the few steps to the garage overhang to fill my basket. But the winter uses them up so quickly. I load them in in threes, in fives, until the orange flames spit and crack in the loose shreds of bark, curling forwards across the stove's brick ceiling to lick yesterday's scribble of blackened sap from the other side of the glass.

93

And yet, somehow through it all I am feeling better. The sickness has almost gone. I can eat everything. I do eat everything. I can look at a cup of coffee now without feeling nauseated. And one afternoon a few days ago it happened. I was kneeling on the rug. I pulled down my sleeve over my hand to grasp the hot iron of the latch and throw the door wide. I stretched out my fingers to the blaze that roared to meet me, almost escaping its dark box. And something moved. The logs inside collapsed in a gust of sparks and settled again with a hiss. And something turned over inside me. For the first time I felt the baby move, like a black butterfly suddenly flexing its wet wings.

I am walking through the city at night. I do walk sometimes, in spite of the danger. Perhaps I court it even, now. Something I've learned from Vic and Steve. The shadows in the alleyways detach themselves from walls, from one another, and I want to introduce myself. I want to become one of them. Instead, I keep walking, head down, measuring my own dark shape on the pavement as it shrinks and grows. But as I pass the Rotonde, I look up. Francis is sitting at a table alone.

He is lit up in the flat glare. The white globe lamps reflect endlessly in the mirror-tiles, an infinitely receding perspective of lit spheres, grouped in threes. His blank expectant stare is repeated endlessly, too. His succession of signet-rings glints on a succession of little fingers. On impulse I go in. 'Hello, Francis.'

He jumps. Then he frowns slightly. He puts the pen he is playing with down on the marble table-top and spreads his hands. 'Sarah. Well met.' At his elbow a paper napkin is covered with squiggles, arrows, a flock of birds wheeling, disappearing against pale sky. Almost like magic a waiter is at his elbow. Francis leans back in his chair. '*Alors, qu'est-ce que tu prends?*' It looks like a gesture of defeat.

'It's all right, I'm not staying. You're waiting for someone.'

Almost imperceptibly he smooths his cuff lower so that it covers his watch. 'No. Really. Please do.'

I raise my eyebrows, but he doesn't try to unsay it. 'If you're sure . . .'

'Of course I'm sure. Don't be absurd.'

'Well, then . . .' I still hesitate. But the waiter is looking at me too curiously. It's too late. 'A coffee, then,' I say quickly. 'Decaff.'

He nods curtly and the man leaves us. We are alone now in the lit space of the window, my own reflection suspended with his between the milky planets. He turns towards me. 'How're the job applications going?'

'They're not.'

'Aren't you putting in for things at home?'

'Oh. Yes. Of course I am. At home. Abroad. But my best chance is still for something here.'

'Ah.' He takes a mouthful of the yellowish liquid in his glass. Yellow Chartreuse? Something more banal? 'What about your own university?' He is still holding the little glass, tapping the base lightly against the surface of the table. The liquid inside shivers in a pattern of concentric rings.

'Oh . . .' I try for a kind of smile. 'I shouldn't think they'd want me. I blotted my copybook there.'

'We all blot our copybooks occasionally.'

'Not in this game, we don't. Once is enough to put you out of the running. One black mark and you can't compete.'

'And you want to compete?'

It's a trick question. I hesitate. He glances down at his watch. I take a quick gulp of my coffee and push the cup away. 'I must go,' I say.

But he puts out a hand and covers mine on the table. It is so unexpected I almost gasp. 'How did you?'

'What?'

'Blot your copybook?'

'Oh . . .' I shake my head, suppressing the laugh that threatens to stop me from giving him a real answer. 'It was a graduate seminar. On a subject quite close to my own field, actually. This guest speaker from Warwick, or somewhere. We'd all had lunch together beforehand. And then suddenly, in the middle of his paper, he turned to me on some small point – asked me to bear him out.'

'And did you?'

'I couldn't.'

'Why not?'

'I didn't know what it was. I hadn't been listening. I'd

started to listen and then I'd drifted off. There was a birch tree outside the window and the leaf-shadows were sort of shivering on the glass. You could see it in the polished table.'

'So what did you say?'

'I said I was sorry. I said I hadn't been listening. I told him it was because of the leaves. And everyone in the room laughed.'

He is still holding my hand. He tightens his grip slightly. 'Sarah . . .' he says.

Our two heads in the dark window are out of focus. The white worlds are fuzzy now at the edges.

'Sarah, I hope you're happy.'

I stare at him. Happy? I haven't thought about it. 'What do you mean?'

He takes back his hand and rubs it across his eyes. When he looks up at me again he seems suddenly tired. 'I hope you're happy, being the kind of person you are.'

'I don't know. Why?' The white spheres are moving now, growing slowly out of the dark spaces of the mirror and passing us in a bright blur. I can almost hear them hum.

'Because if *you*'re not happy, being the kind of person you are,' Francis says slowly, 'there's no help for the rest of us.' I blink quickly and the white expanse of the Rotonde slips back into place, the grouped spheres slow gently to a stop. I push back my chair. As I leave I almost collide with Lervain, standing with his back to me just outside the door, the familiar hang of his fawn raincoat flattened slightly against the glass.

Steve and Vic were what you would call buddies. They had a whole male-buddy life together that I didn't know about. Sometimes I used to mention something, a film that had sounded worth seeing, a place I wouldn't have minded going to visit, and they used to glance at each other with just the slightest suspicion of a grin. 'Have you been there?' I used to say, or, 'Have you seen it already?'

'Well, not really *been*, not properly.' Vic used to sit staring down at his hands. Steve used to look faintly guilty. 'We did just run out there briefly, the other Thursday. But we didn't have time to see much. We could always go again.'

And then we *would* go again, the three of us. Romanesque

churches, a moated castle where the weeds grew as high as a man's head. You should have seen us. I used to sit on my own under the restored arches, or among the Louis XVI chairs in the dining-hall, as the chamber musicians sweated their way through Albinoni or Haydn. And when I went out into the sunlit courtyard I used to find Vic and Steve perched side by side on the lip of a stone fountain, smoking, sharing some private joke. Or in the cinema, they would be laughing at things they knew were coming. At moments of suspense they used to look at me sideways to see how I was taking it. In weepies they used to point at me and grin.

And people started coming up to us. At night, as we walked back through the dark streets. They'd hear us speaking English and come up behind us and catch one of the men by the sleeve. Vic, particularly. Sometimes it felt as if everyone in the city knew him, as if he had friends in every quarter.

The transactions took place quickly. Not as furtively as you might have imagined. Not in alleys, or urine-stained door-ways, or among the rotting paraphernalia of a piece of waste-ground. But in the usual back streets, in a half-dark that was actually very ordinary. A quick exchange of voices, just words spoken normally. I couldn't even hear what language they were in. Vic used to get out his money and count it out and groan under his breath. A small packet of something. Out of the corner of my eye I would catch him slipping it into his pocket.

Sometimes it was in daylight, even. Once a guy with a pony-tail ran out from a café terrace and chased after us with cubes of sugar. It looked to me like some kind of joke.

And every day they were meeting new people. A weird international crowd that hung around someone called Carol, who lived with three other girls on the ground floor of a big house somewhere out in the suburbs. I could imagine it. A gang of them sitting on the floor, hardly speaking. Joss-sticks. Candles. The guitars propped in a corner, against the wall. 'You should come with us,' Steve said to me. 'It's great. You'd like them all.'

'Why would I?'

These days when he came to see me he always came alone. And even then he came only rarely. We never played cards any more. He never told me jokes. One by one the reiterated punchlines had begun to fall flat. 'Because. Try it. It would do you good.'

'I can't.'

'Why not?'

'I'm reading.'

'About cockroaches?'

'Yes!'

'Shit-face. Is that all you ever . . . ?'

I went up to him where he lay on my bed and tried to thump him. He held my wrists, laughing. But I broke free and pushed. He fell off the bed obligingly, and lay there on the floor, still rolling from side to side with laughter. And then I started to kick him, hard, harder, my shoe coming down on his thin ribs over and over again, until suddenly he caught at my ankle and I toppled over, falling on top of him, half-winded. 'Sarah, you're coming,' he said. 'Like it or not. It's no good. They've got it all planned. It's a birthday party. For you. You've got to come.' I raised my head and looked at him. 'Who told you it was my birthday?'

'You did.'

I was going to scream. I was going to yank his pale hair out in handfuls. But he caught my head between his hands and pulled me down and filled my mouth with his tongue.

The night of the party it was unseasonably warm. We threw off our jackets inside the metal box of the van. There was a girl with us, Lisa, someone Vic had bumped into somewhere, a plump, pretty *au pair* from Tamworth. They treated her quite differently from how they treated me, I noticed. On the surface they seemed kinder. And the conversation came and went like some kind of stylised dance – fingertips just touching, a half-ludicrous curtsey. A veiled smile, a discreet toss of the head. Where did she learn that? But the words themselves never quite met.

In the back of the van Lisa was sitting on the only cushion. I squatted over the wheel. My legs were braced against the metal ridges of the floor, sliding away from under me at each sudden turn. Once my upper arm met hers in a suck of hot flesh. We laughed and screamed. Steve only drove faster.

98

When we hit a particularly large bump, Vic turned his head to check on us, and grinned.

I strained to see where we were going, but it was impossible. How could I match that reeling fragment of street and frontage to any vaguely remembered map of the city I might have had in my head? Finally we drew to a halt. Steve got out and ran round to the back. He threw open the metal doors and electric light flooded in, across where we half-lay, spreadeagled in a hot heap. He was still laughing. He helped Lisa out. I jumped to the ground after her. I remember bending my knees like a child jumping from a tree. I was feeling slightly sick.

'This is it.' We walked through a high green metal gate into a square front garden dominated by a single tree, some odd kind of tree I haven't met anywhere else, before or since, the branches growing outwards and downwards from the central trunk, sloping gently almost to meet the ground. You could just see an old rope-ladder dangling from somewhere inside the thickest part of it, trailing down almost to the bare earth. You could imagine its treads worn with the feet of a succession of children, its ropes darkened by months of rain and frost.

The entrance to the ground-floor flat seemed to be at the back. We trooped round, along a narrow path between clumps of overgrown garden, and through a door which led directly into the kitchen. A big old black stove, a tiled floor. Big pans in different colours of chipped enamel.

And beyond it a large empty room with a bare wooden floor. It was just like the room I'd imagined. There were the party guests – still standing, true, but a bit unsteady already. You could almost see the paper cups going soft and porous in their hands. Candles everywhere, of every possible shape and size, almost too many to count. The joss-sticks, in a narrow chipped vase on the mantelpiece. And there were the guitars – Steve's, and another, flashier instrument that must have belonged to Carol, over in the far corner, leaning against the wall.

A young woman came forward to meet us. She took our coats and disappeared. She must have been taking them into a bedroom. She was wearing something dark under an even darker shawl with long fringes, and a long patterned skirt.

When she moved I could see that her feet were bare. 'Sarah. We meet at last. Happy birthday.' I can still hear her saying it. Private school, ponies, a nanny, probably.

I swallowed. 'Actually, it's tomorrow.'

Steve said, 'But Carol thought Saturday would be better. There's even a cake.'

She guided me back to the kitchen, her hand lightly on my elbow. There on the counter was this huge creation. Like something a child might have made – all sponge-cake and pink icing. You could see where it had sunk in the middle and someone had tried to hide it under a pile of strawberries. Twenty-five pink candles. 'You'll have to cut it, later, when everyone's here. We can turn out the lights, and sing, and think of England.'

'I wouldn't want to spoil anything.' I think that was what I said.

The big room was filling up steadily. French people, Belgians, Americans. An Australian guy who seemed to want to talk about wind-surfing. A tall young Swedish-speaking Finn who looked over my head and quoted MacNeice. And I was speaking several languages, more and more effortlessly with the wine. By the time it ran out I seemed to be understanding them all.

Then people began to drift off, leaving, or huddling in corners. The light dimmed as the candles burned out one by one. The air was almost unbreathable – fogged and yet at the same time sharp with smoke. The music was louder. Or softer. I could hardly tell which.

Outside I nearly bumped into Lisa. She was standing near the doorway, next to a puddle of vomit. In the faint glow from the open door I could see that her face was streaked with mascara. Crying, obviously. I found my way round to the front, floundering through the web of branches, covering my eyes with my hands until I came to the clear space in the centre. I leaned back against the twisted trunk and looked up at the stars, taking great gulps of the warm damp air. The constellations began to spin slowly in their basket of black twigs. Then I climbed the ladder. I sat there for a long time, my feet on the top rung, the tree matted and swaying under me like some apology for a thatched roof.

I climbed down awkwardly and went back in. By that time the main room was in almost total darkness, the smoke was heavier than ever. I felt my way through to the hall and started opening doors at random. A tiny bedroom hardly bigger than a pantry. Another with two beds in it. The toilet. A bathroom with a cracked tub. A cupboard full of trunks and suitcases. And one last door, slightly open. I went to put my hand on the knob and almost tripped over something. It felt like a bundle of rags. I looked down, screwing up my eyes to make out what it was. It was Vic.

'You can't go in there, Sarah.' He was looking up at me. I could see the whites of his eyes in the crack of light from the door.

'Why not?'

He shrugged. But he reached up for the handle and pulled the door shut with a little click. We were in darkness.

'I'm leaving. I need to get my jacket.'

'Why don't you just . . .'

But already I was elbowing past him. I wrenched the handle out of his hand and pushed the door open. The bedside lamp was on, turned at an odd angle to cast its patterned halo across the ceiling. Carol naked, face downwards on the bed, her hair across the pillow, just a body. And Steve on top of her, with his jeans still round his thighs in a heave of pocket-studs and carriers and belt-buckle. Above them his white buttocks, the dents coming and going. Doing it on a pile of coats. I could see the sleeve of my jacket trailing from the end of the bed, almost under his left ankle. I stepped forwards and pulled it out from underneath. They didn't seem to notice. They didn't seem to be aware even that someone had entered the room.

I pushed past Vic in the doorway. He pulled the door to again behind me, shutting out the light. I could feel him laughing beside me. 'I'm leaving,' I said again.

'How will you get back?'

'I'll walk.'

'Do you know the way?'

'I'll find it.' I swung my jacket up and over my shoulders. 'I just turn out of here and keep going, right? And eventually I'll come to something that looks familiar.'

'It must be six miles.'

'So? What do you suggest?'

He didn't answer. I turned away from him. I made for the bright bulb in the kitchen, through fog. The birthday cake was still in its place on the counter. I noticed the candles were leaning slightly outwards at odd angles. The icing under them was getting soft. And someone had got there before me. Someone had scrawled 'Fuck off' across the pink surface with the end of a blunt knife.

The city was in darkness. There was only the odd light to guide me through the streets. There were wide, almost featureless stretches dotted with two- and three-storey villas. I could almost feel the families asleep under the tiles, in the thick dark. I passed the occasional low hangar-like structure – agricultural machinery or light industry. Here and there a garage – Total, Esso. Cars parked diagonally under a row of trees. And then, as I got close to the centre, the tighter streets of shops and shuttered windows. Suddenly, a square.

I hardly met anyone. A woman hurrying home, her handbag clutched to her side, her face lowered. A pair of young men, staggering, their arms round each other's necks. Once, a kerb-crawler, slowing as I slowed, changing into second gear as I quickened my pace. I turned into a one-way street to lose him and kept walking.

And then quite suddenly I came out into a part I knew. The market square. The gutters were still full of decaying orange-peel, the bruised outer leaves of vegetables. From the top of its short flight of steps the cathedral was facing me, its high black door closed. In my mind's eye I could still almost see that awful exhibition of wartime photographs, the whites of the eyes just faintly lighter than the rubble. The floodlights must have gone off hours ago. Above my head the sky was so dark I could hardly even make out the sharp slope of the roof. I felt a spot of rain on the back of my hand.

And then the sky opened. The drops became a deluge, the first tentative patter a steady drumming on asphalt and stone. I pulled my jacket round me, but the water ran down inside my collar. My skirt was sticking to my thighs. Water from my wet fringe ran across my face so that I could hardly see. But by that time I knew where I was going. Head down, I ran the last few hundred metres to the familiar block of flats where I lived in my little rented room. The concierge must have been asleep. I hung on the automatic buzzer until the front door swung open. I pushed through into the ground-floor passage. My feet clattered on the tiles. Water still dripped into my eyes as I bent and fumbled for my key.

I reached for the switch just inside and turned on the light. I blinked. Something wasn't quite right, the books on my work-table had been almost imperceptibly reshuffled. By the chest-of-drawers, there was the squashed body of a cockroach, on its back. I picked it up and deposited it in the metal waste-bin. The top left-hand drawer wasn't quite flush, the foot of a pair of tights dangling. I poked the shred of nylon in with my finger and pushed the drawer to. Then I thought better of it. I pulled it open, felt under a pile of underwear for my passport, opened it for the slim wad of 10-franc notes I was saving to pay my fare home.

Gone. Predictably. I held the passport by its two covers and shook it. Nothing fell out. I closed it and replaced it at the bottom of the drawer.

Then I went to the window. It was slightly open, as I had left it. But the shutters I always closed carefully and bolted. Now a strip of black was just visible between them, perhaps half an inch wide. The latch hung loose. I examined them closely. The lip of one of the vents next to the latch had been pulled slightly out of shape, as if someone had widened it, penetrated it with a thin instrument, the blade of a knife, perhaps. The paint on the latch itself was scraped away on one side. I looked down and saw that the yellowish dust on the floor was patterned with footprints. My own. Or were some of them larger? If I looked closely I might be able to see where a man's toe had first touched the floor, where he had doubled back on himself, where he had rocked once on the ball of his foot before climbing back on to the sill on his way out.

I closed the shutters, and then the window. The long walk had sobered me up almost completely. And now this. I dried my hair slowly on a towel. I didn't bother to get undressed. I only kicked off my shoes. Then I slid down into the bed with all my clothes on, and pulled the covers up to my ears. I lay there, shivering slightly, watching the slits in the shutters go from blue to pale grey to white with the morning, until the sun finally rose over the ugly concrete buildings that backed on to the courtyard. And that was it. There I was. I don't know what you would call it, really. Not tricked, exactly. Just wondering if he really ever was kind, or if I was only stupid. Trapped under those bars of light.

Mid-January. The days are getting longer now. Already the night is shrinking back into itself, the hours of daylight gradually stretching. I wake in the morning and see that it is no longer pitch black. If I try hard enough I can just make out the small square of the window in its thick embrasure, the shape of my sweatshirt draped over the one chair, the shadowy space under the slope of the ceiling where I shall put the cot.

But it is colder than ever. Rain, then sleet. A wind that cuts me to the bone even in the few minutes it takes to cross the gravel and unlock my car, a wind that howls in the trees at night-time. Puddles everywhere, soaking my feet when I go to empty the rubbish. Mud to my ankles. Then the pond freezes. The ducks swim in ever smaller circles. The puddles are iced over, trapping air in delicate patterns like white wings.

I pile logs in the woodstove. I wait for it to snow. One of these days it will. The sky is a uniform grey. You would think it was full of the stuff. One evening I turn on the radio and hear that it has been snowing all round us, in other places. In the Alps, the Ardennes, the Pyrenees. In Bavaria. In the Pas de Calais. In England, even. I tell myself it is only a matter of time.

And I miss you so terribly. Hardly even a matter of days since the real sickness ended, and now this other sickness swells to take its place. When I go out to my car, Dominique is waiting to waylay me. She looks sceptically at the briefcase, the bursting folders held together with elastic, the piles of books from the departmental library. 'Research?' she says. Her voice has a sarcastic edge to it, tart. Almost a kind of challenge.

'Research.'

'*Tu as tort, tu sais. Il faudrait . . .*'

'*Oh, vous savez . . .*' I bundle my things into the back seat, without meeting her eyes.

As I drive away she mouths something at me through the glass. I lean over and roll down the nearside window, but I only catch the tail end of it. '. . . by the chimney?' she says.

'What?'

'Is it all right if Robert just goes in and stacks some wood inside, by the chimney?'

I'm touched by her kindness. 'You know . . .' I call out to her. 'You deserve something better, a less bad-tempered tenant than I am.'

But she only grins. 'You pay your rent on time, don't you? That's all that matters.' As I swing out into the lane I see her turn her back on me and go in.

And sometimes I think it is only the woodstove that keeps me here through this weather, away from the easier life of the town with its underfloor heating and bulbous radiators, from the temptation of jacking this all in and buying a plane ticket. One night I pile the iron chamber so full of wood it roars like a small firestorm, as if it could suck in my whole life, its whole improbable population of foreigners. When the wood has crumbled almost to nothing I open the door and lie down on the rug in front of it. I find myself staring into its red eye. Your tape is playing, the one I always hated.

> *Chaque nuit le même songe m'épouvante.*
> *Toujours une voix grave et lente*
> *Me répète ces mots:*
> *« Un enfant vient de naître*
> *Qui fera disparaître*
> *Ton trône et ton pouvoir . . . »*

And it still doesn't snow. Perhaps it is snowing, where you are. I close my eyes and suck on my own hand, as if it were yours, as if it were part of you.

One Friday afternoon, as I come along the corridor towards 107, Laurence is waiting for me outside the door.

'*Madame . . .*'

'Call me Sarah,' I say.

She finds it difficult to wrap her mouth round the syllables. 'Sarah . . .' Her thin hand is resting on the wall, half-supporting

her weight, the long fingers like the bones in a bird's spread
wing. She doesn't seem to have any books with her.

'Yes?'

'May I speak to you for a moment?'

I am surprised: until now she has hardly spoken, hardly
given any real impression of herself at all. 'Of course.'

'I wanted to make my excuses.' She flicks the shiny hair
back with a little movement of her head. 'I'm too busy to come
to your class. I have too much work.'

'Thank you for telling me. If you want to know what we're
doing next week . . .'

'I mean, *all* of your classes.'

I feel myself start to blush. 'Don't you think some of the
spoken idioms might be . . . ?'

She smiles faintly. She takes her hand from the wall and
stands up straight. She is a good ten centimetres taller than I
am. 'But I meet the familiar locutions also, in my reading.'

I hesitate. 'Does it matter to anyone if you don't come?'

'M. Lervain knows about it. He is helping me with my
paper. It was his suggestion, in fact – a way of creating time.'

'Oh, well . . . If he knows about it . . .'

She lifts her head and smiles at me. 'Perhaps we can meet
in other circumstances, outside? I would welcome the opportunity of knowing you.' She is so thin. And these days I am
already getting heavier, my waist beginning to thicken under
the sweater. She seems to look right through me. *Does she
know?* But surely. I have been so careful these last months,
biting back the waves of sickness, working harder than ever,
wearing make-up so no one would think me pale. Could she
possibly have seen through all that?

'I'm sorry to lose you,' I tell her. 'Of course. But I'm sure
we'll bump into each other, as you say.'

The *maîtrise* class seems smaller without her. I look round to
see if anyone else is missing, but they are all there – Jean-Luc,
Philippe and the gang. Denise, with the squeaky voice and
freckles. Serge, leaning back in his chair, his long legs stretched
half across the aisle, his pocked skin gleaming against even
teeth. Marthe, not looking at me. I open my file and pull out
the sheaf of marked translations. I raise my voice just enough

to reach to the back right-hand corner of the room, where she is sitting. I say, 'You excelled yourselves this last week.'

The first hour passes quickly. We go through the translation, teasing one another a little, trying on the different alternatives, everyone chipping in. Some of the suggestions are outrageous. It's Friday afternoon, after all. Language is a funny business. By three o'clock we have a fair copy written on the blackboard, each fragment chalked up in a different handwriting. I read it through slowly. It seems to hang together. And they have copied it down. Only Marthe sits with her arms folded.

She says suddenly, 'Don't you think this is a pretty sterile exercise?'

The others look up and start to smile at one another. 'What do you mean, "sterile"?' I ask her.

'Well . . . Not very useful. Proscriptive. Simplistic. Don't you think translation can be more creative than that?'

I say carefully, 'It *can* . . . Of course it can. But in a class-room, where we're all–'

She interrupts me. 'We're not all *anything*! Aren't you robbing the whole thing of the one individual spark that can make translation meaningful?'

'Am I?'

She looks at me. 'I think you are.'

'Could you do better?'

I expect her to stand up and shout at me, *Yes!* But she shakes her head. She is angry. 'Oh no. You don't put that on me. We're only the students.' Her voice is shaking, her mouth tense with sarcasm. 'The glory and the responsibility are all yours.'

The class is restless now, the initial amusement shifting towards boredom in a clatter of books and feet. For a moment I think they are walking out on me. Then I see they have the regulation grammar-books open in front of them, at the page where we left off last week. Without being asked, Jean-Luc reads out the first sentence: ' "*She dare not say it.*" ' He seems to consider. ' "Daren't she say it?" ' He looks up at me and winks.

Somehow the second hour passes. Under the desk, surrep-titiously, I glance at my watch. The minute hand seems hardly to move. The students are dutiful and unresponsive now, answering me in as few words as they can get away with.

Only Marthe is voluble, contesting every point.

'*Why* do you say "When I leave", and not "When I shall leave"?'

'I don't know. We just do. It isn't just me. I have it on good authority.' I pick up my *Grammaire anglaise de l'Etudiant* and tap the page with my forefinger.

'It isn't logical.'

'Language isn't always logical. Didn't anyone tell you? Language a living thing is.' I catch Denise's eye. She is trying not to groan. She picks up her pen and starts to doodle furiously in the margin of a piece of squared paper. Serge yawns loudly. Jean-Luc is staring up at the ceiling. 'If you don't believe me,' I say, 'go and ask someone else. One of the *lecteurs*. Or Dr Stillwood. Or M. Lervain. The whole thing's riddled with incongruities, rules that are made to be broken, *faux amis* . . .'

'*Faux amis?*'

'You know. Words that look as if they ought to mean the same thing in both languages, but don't. Like "*terrible*" and "terrible".'

'Like "ignore" and "*ignorer*",' Philippe says. He turns round in his seat to look at her.

' "*Conscience*" and "conscience".'

' "*Assister*", "assist".'

'"*Misère*".' It is Serge's voice, slightly sleepy.

' "*Gentil*",' I say, without looking at Marthe. ' "Gentle".'

She looks back at me without blinking. ' "*Sentiment*",' she says quietly. ' "Sentiment"; "sentimental".' It is a challenge. She pushes back her chair and stands up, bundling her papers together into the old briefcase. Then she gives us all a quick nod and makes for the door.

One afternoon as I am walking out to my car, I meet Lervain. My head is bent against the icy wet wind that plays round the pale concrete buildings, whipping up small tornadoes of dead leaves and litter, the usual files clutched in my arms, my car key dangling from one finger. I almost bump right into him. He puts out both hands and steadies me. I take a step backwards.

'Sarah!' He looks almost dashing, a soft check scarf over a thigh-length winter coat.

'I'm on my way home. I've just finished.' In spite of myself, my voice sounds somehow edgy with guilt.

'I was hoping I might run into you.'

'Oh?'

He is looking decidedly pleased with himself. Smug, almost. 'A piece of good news.'

'Yes?'

'I've just been investigating the financial options, for next year. It seems there's money available for an associate senior lectureship. And with your Ph.D., you'd be eligible. I'm sure something can be arranged.'

I don't quite trust him. 'Really?'

'Well, the money's there, apparently. And it seems no other department's put in for it. And you *are*, *theoretically* . . .'

'Yes,' I say. Along the path in front of me a cold eddy picks up a small spiral of brownish debris and deposits it at my feet. 'Yes, *theoretically*, I suppose I am.'

'So, you'll accept it? If I can pin them down, you'll be quite happy to stay on with us?'

'Of course.'

'You've been doing such wonderful things with the students. Don't think I haven't noticed.' He reaches out and pats me on the shoulder. 'And you're so much more use to us now than . . .'

'Are there other people?'

'Oh . . . Not really. I shouldn't worry about that, if I were you. The suggestions they've made us from England are really quite unsuitable. A woman with a young child! *Figurez-vous!* Now, what would a department like ours do with someone like that?'

I look at him. 'I don't know.'

'Precisely.'

'But what about your *maîtrise* students? Some of them must be going on to take the *Aggrég*. Don't they come into the reckoning at all?'

He shrugs. 'We're pretty much bound by the rules. We're not really free to employ them. Unless someone were to drop out at very short notice, for personal reasons, or illness. Then, perhaps . . .'

'Laurence Chaulieux,' I say to him.

His eyes narrow slightly. 'Poor girl. She hasn't been too well lately. She's got very thin. And she's very good. The sensitivity there is quite amazing. That rich inner life. But until they're *aggrégés,* we're not really allowed . . .'

'Quite.'

'So . . . Anyway . . . It looks very hopeful. I'm keeping my fingers crossed.'

'Thank you.'

'I do appreciate it, the way you've been quietly building up the department's resources on your own initiative, the energy you've put into all that.'

'I did it for my own satisfaction. And for the students. I care about the students.'

'I know you do.'

'I wanted to do well by them.'

'And you have. You have.' He waves his hands airily. 'And they must all be very appreciative too.'

There is something in his expression that isn't quite natural, an odd tension about the eyebrows. Is he laughing at me? 'Some of them are,' I say.

'I imagine all of them are.' Now one eyebrow is raised. The irony is becoming overt.

'Yes,' I tell him. Two can play at this game. 'I imagine that too.'

And Laurence Chaulieux is ever less visible. It seems that I was just the precursor: one by one she has let all her classes slip. Sometimes I catch a fleeting glimpse of her, hurrying, huddled into her coat against the rain.

More often it is only her name I catch: '*Cette petite Chaulieux . . .*' I am in the English staffroom, turning the silky pages of a dictionary with one finger. I don't look up.

'Is she having problems?' It is Francis Stillwood's voice, clear and serious. 'Is there something I should know about?'

'Oh . . .' Lervain is half-laughing. I feel the table shake. 'I had a little chat with her the other afternoon, about her paper. She's deep into it now. Metaphors of time and death in the last plays. You should have heard her. It was quite something. All these appalling words, all these terrifying concepts coming from the mouth of this young, golden . . . There's no doubt about it, she's an extraordinary little thing.'

In spite of myself, I glance up. I am just quick enough to see that the first look on Francis's face is one of distaste. Then his face goes flat, the first reaction wiped out. He runs his hand through his hair. 'I don't think she's well,' he says.

'From which point of view? Physical? Or psychological?'

'God! How should I know? Perhaps both. She's got so thin. Is she eating?'

'She's certainly devouring the words.'

'That's what I'm afraid of.'

'We'll see at the Departmental Dinner, perhaps. You can shadow her and report back.' The table shakes again. The sensitive pages of the dictionary shiver, still open at *rhétoricien; rien; rieur.*

There is a silence. I look up again. Francis is staring out of the window, his grey eyes hardly blinking. He seems to be watching the sluggish procession of clouds outside. The lights are on, the heavy winter sky bluish, his face reflected in gold in the glass. 'Is she friendly with any of the *lecteurs,* do you know? That might . . .'

I hear Lervain's dry laugh. '*C'est un esprit pur. Qu'est-ce que tu veux?'*

Suddenly they seem to become aware of me, in my dark corner. Lervain clears his throat. Then he pushes his chair back, busily collecting up his belongings. He takes down his coat and scarf from the hook on the back of the door.

'*Allez, à demain, Francis. Mademoiselle.'* He nods to us both and backs out through the open door.

We wait for the click as it shuts. We look at each other. Francis sighs, shaking his head slowly. Then he gets up and goes to the window. He stands there with his back to me, his hands in his pockets. When I close the dictionary and stand up to put it back on the shelf behind me he doesn't look round.

It is a pleasant enough restaurant they have chosen. White tablecloths. Pink linen napkins. An almost daunting array of cutlery. And the glasses fine-stemmed and gleaming: small for the white, larger for the red, flutes for the dessert champagne.

We are all dressed up to the nines, Mireille in a floaty white blouse and soft skirt in a subtle feathery fabric of beige and silver, Francis in a green jacket that looks as if it's made of some mixture of linen and silk. I sit facing the window, a view that in summer would be over the garden, curtailed now by the darkness. Just a few bright metres of cold grass, the skeleton of a climbing vine at the edges of the frame. The place is owned by Lervain's younger brother, someone said. He made his money in Calvados. He comes out briefly from somewhere in the back reaches of the kitchen and bows to us, each in turn. He leans across the table to shake hands with Paul and Francis, kisses Mireille on both cheeks as if he has known her for years. He looks a bit like a younger version of Lervain himself, in dinner-jacket and gleaming white shirt. Fewer wrinkles, slightly more hair. A general air of that enjoyment of life which I suddenly realise Lervain himself lacks.

It was Francis's idea, apparently, to invite the graduate students this year, for the first time. They make a lively group, on a separate table slightly in front of us and to the left. Out of the corner of my eye I can just see Jean-Luc, his expression of suppressed laughter. For a moment Serge blocks my view, leaning forwards to pour himself a full glass of wine. He slops it slightly as he raises it to his mouth. They have brought their *Restau U* manners with them. They will be pounding out tattoos on their plates and throwing bread at one another before the end.

Only Marthe has chosen to sit with us. And she is mute, her face lowered to her plate. She looks uncomfortable, in a dress. An antique necklace she touches almost constantly. I find myself wondering where she got it. The glass of the long windows is ever darker, veering towards midnight blue. The wrought links slip in and out between her fingers like worry-beads, or a kind of game.

She is sitting opposite me; Francis is to her left. He runs one finger round the rim of his empty glass, then looks up and smiles. 'Where's Laurence?' I ask him. 'Isn't she here?'

'She isn't well, Sarah. She sent her apologies.'

'Is it something serious?'

'No, I don't think so.' He flashes a sideways look at Marthe. 'No, I'm sure it isn't. A small digestive upset, she said.'

112

'There's some bug going round.'

'Have you had it?'

'*Me?*'

Marthe looks up.

'No, I . . .' I say.

'Only I thought you'd been seeming a bit under the weather lately.'

There is a waitress behind us, reaching between us with oval silver dishes of cold meat and shredded celeriac and *cornichons*. Lervain is filling our glasses. In the centre of the table, on a white plate, is a mound of paté, a miniature volcano garnished with something green that could be chervil. It looks oddly amateurish. Then I remember. It is the departmental tradition. Lervain has made it himself, a gesture of thanks for another year's hard work and faithful service, perhaps even slightly ironic. Or perhaps it is some intimate joke between him and his kid brother, still vying for excellence in a few chosen skills. Perhaps the brother is a secret dabbler in the idioms of literary criticism. Perhaps there is a whole Lervain tribe, rich with unlikely talents.

'Have some.' Francis passes me the plate. I take the smallest lump on my knife and smear it on a piece of bread. But it is unexpectedly good. I come back for more. Everyone is eating it, with obvious enjoyment. The mound rapidly diminishes. The level of the wine in our glasses has dropped noticeably, too. Marthe takes the last small scrapings and leans back, looking at the wall over my head. She says nothing. The necklace has left a small red mark on the side of her neck, like a scratch. She looks at me and raises her glass.

The table has gone silent, as if by tacit consent. For a moment I am puzzled. There is a kind of generalised embarrassment, something that seems to float in the air just above our heads. And then I realise why – the simple words of appreciation, the basic kindness that no one here will stoop to utter. It is almost palpable. We are all only thinking of our stomachs, but no one will give Lervain the satisfaction of praise.

And suddenly I feel exasperated for him. He is too powerful. Democratically elected or not, he has put himself in the position of someone who can make or break other lives. And if he makes good pâté, no one will tell him. That simple kindness is out of his reach.

The conversation has picked up again now. All around me the voices have sprung up, almost simultaneous. The incongruous topics vie with one another for dominance. I wipe my mouth carefully on my napkin. I pick up my glass and take a big gulp of wine. I put my glass down and wipe my mouth again.

Lervain is sitting at my right elbow. I turn to watch his guarded profile until I succeed in catching his eye. He swivels slightly in his chair and bends his head to hear what I am going to tell him. 'The pâté was wonderful – absolutely delicious,' I say.

His face brightens, like a boy's. 'Did you think so?'

'How did you make it?'

'Oh, you know . . . Chicken or rabbit livers, a bit of thyme, *crème fraîche*, a dash of the old family *Calva*. It's easy. I could show you.'

'No breadcrumbs?'

He laughs. 'No breadcrumbs.'

'No trade secrets?'

He is beaming at me. 'Just practice. No secrets. You know me, I don't believe in mystifications.'

'No?'

'You can ask Francis . . .' He looks round at them all for corroboration – Francis, Mireille, Paul. Even Marthe comes within the general benign sweep of his hand.

I follow his gesture. They are all looking at me. And it is then that I become aware of our own voices, of how loud they sounded. Everyone is listening, not just on our own table but on the other table as well. People have actually stopped eating to listen to us. For perhaps a minute already the only conversation in the whole room has been ours.

But it passes. Gradually the exchanges resume. We move on to the next course, and the next. The wines succeed one another. We graduate to the big glasses. The faces, in the lamplight, are rosy. I am holding back, though. Since that first liberating glass of white I have drunk hardly anything. Something is warning me to stay sober as all around me the others eat and drink steadily, familiar with these periodic excesses

114

almost since childhood, as used to them as they are to life itself.

And now we have finally reached the cheese. Lervain passes it with a little flourish to Mireille. She takes a sliver of Chaource, hardly more than a crumb of Roquefort. She slides the plate across to Francis. I watch him take a modest wedge of *chèvre*. Opposite me Marthe is raising the bottle of red wine.

She pours it into each glass in turn. Francis's, to her left. Only a few drops, and he waves his hand at her to stop. Mireille's, almost to the brim. Lervain's, with a nod. For no obvious reason she misses me out and goes on to Paul. 'A toast,' she says.

Lervain barely looks up.

'To the Department.'

'And all who sail in her.' Francis makes no attempt to raise his glass.

But the others have raised theirs, as if by reflex. Mireille, Paul. Finally even Lervain himself. I look down at my own glass. Its emptiness seems to cry out to the whole table. To Marthe in particular. I feel ridiculous. I have nothing to raise, no toast to drink, no department to sail in. I am glaring at her, but she is looking elsewhere, half-turned towards the students' table behind her, as if for an audience. 'Could I have some wine, please?' I say.

She doesn't seem to hear me. No one hears me. It is as if I weren't even there, as if I were sick or had already left them, my place taken by a ghost. I could shout at them and no one would hear me. Through a haze of lamplight I see her turn to Lervain. 'So what made you first decide you wanted to study English?' she asks him.

He seems to recoil slightly. She hasn't called him '*Monsieur*', she hasn't even bothered to smile. 'I was in Corsica,' he says. 'Under a fig-tree, reading Lawrence.'

'And you?' She has turned to Paul.

'Me?' Paul says. 'I was in England. Oddly enough. In Brighton. Sitting under the pier with a girl called Stephanie.'

'Doing a crossword, no doubt,' Mireille says.

'What about you?'

'Oh . . . I was already doing English and German when I met Paul.'

'Dr Stillwood? What made you decide on French?'

'Actually, I didn't. I read English.' Francis shakes his head. 'I'm something of an anomaly here.'

'So what brought you to France?'

'Ah . . .' He is uncharacteristically nervous, playing with his signet-ring, pulling it up towards the joint and then letting it slip back, over and over again. 'That's a long story. I rather like Paul's scenario. A girl under the pier. Doing crosswords. I think I might be able to relate to that.' He takes a quick gulp of wine, and wipes his mouth on the back of his hand. Uncharacteristic. Now his glass is as empty as my own.

She doesn't ask me. No one asks me. I might not be there. Then Lervain says, almost aggressively, 'And you?'

I jump. For a moment I think the question is levelled at me. But no. It is Marthe he is addressing. She leans forward, resting her wrists on the edge of the table. She spreads her fingers on either side of her plate. 'Me? I haven't chosen anything definitively.'

He almost barks, 'Then what are you doing here?'

'Learning.'

'Learning what?'

'Learning what not to choose.'

He grunts. 'And when do you expect the decision to be . . . made?'

'I have no idea. When I'm about your age?' She looks suddenly directly at him, as if she is concentrating on something, listening to something we aren't any of us really aware of. I am watching her. I can hardly believe what I'm hearing. 'When I'm just about over my midlife crisis, and the possibilities are fewer. When there's not so much to lose.'

There is an uncomfortable silence. Then Paul steps into the gap. He starts to laugh loudly. 'So that's what it was,' he says, 'under the pier at Brighton! My midlife crisis! No wonder the old equipment's never been quite the same since!' He reaches behind me and touches Lervain's shoulder. '*Attention, mon vieux!* All that rain does strange things to the system, those boiled potatoes, that *spotted Dick.*'

They are all drunk. Or is Paul only pretending? I see Lervain steady himself slightly on the edge of the table as he stands up. He almost trips on a chair-leg. Francis follows him to the cloakroom, his own face slightly flushed.

I reach out then for the wine bottle. I turn it towards me so I can read the label. Beaune, with the Tastevin seal on it. There is about a glass left. I pour it into my own and sip it slowly. I lean forward to meet her across the table. '*Chapeau*,' I say to her, under my breath.

She hates me. She always has. Drunk or sober, she will always do this, wherever we are. For a moment it is almost as if I can feel the sickness returning, the foetus inside me a small flower of frantically multiplying cells, the stem writhing fast-forward towards sunlight in a clip from some natural history sequence. She hates everyone. Whatever she is learning, it is not kindness. Not happiness, either. Whatever she is learning, from me or from any of us, it is not something I can ever teach.

They bring us the desserts – little pastry cases of jellied fruit, sorbet, some banana and chocolate creation. Lervain seems to have left. Francis, too. No one feels like opening the champagne.

I go back with Paul and Mireille, in their car. Paul is driving. He hasn't actually drunk much, I realise, though Mireille has probably had enough for both of them. The roads are almost deserted. Paul turns his headlights on full, a white path into nothing. And from the white air in front of us small snowflakes rush at the windscreen to be flattened under the wipers like moths.

I am in the back. In front of me Paul's greying head and Mireille's ginger halo, almost the same colour now in the darkness. From time to time she leans over towards him and tries to rest her head on his shoulder. He pushes her away. 'Don't do that! I can't change gear, for God's sake!' But his voice is good-humoured. There is affection in it. 'If you can't behave, I'll make you change places with Sarah and sit in the back.'

But Mireille only turns round to look at me. 'Sarah, do you *want* to sit in the front? Is this making you feel sick?'

'What do you mean?'

'Well, don't you get car-sick?'

'Oh, that. Yes. Sometimes.'

'Would you feel better in the front?'

'No. I'm all right. Honestly.'

117

She has twisted round to face me, her arm along the top of the seat and her chin resting on it. 'Are you sure?'

'Honestly.'

It isn't honest at all: just turning to look at her, at any point of reference inside the car, has made my stomach start to churn. Something hot rises under my ribs. I can't talk to people in cars. I turn away from her to the window. I open it a fraction at the top and the cold air leaks in on to my face. I close my eyes.

When I open them she has turned back to the road. All I can see is an hourglass of white screen between the black shapes of their two heads. Then, without any warning, Mireille says, 'Sarah, why did Joseph leave?'

I wind the window down further. Tiny snowflakes sting my face like a handful of fine sand. I take a deep breath. I wind the glass up again. 'I don't know. He wanted to.'

'He could have stayed on another year. I thought he was going to. I thought that's what he'd decided.'

'Yes. So did I.'

'Did you fall out, the two of you? Was that the reason?'

'I don't know,' I say again. 'Not really. I think he just felt . . . that things had changed, and that he didn't want to stay. I think he suddenly saw he'd made the wrong decision. I think he just felt it was time to leave.'

'And you haven't split up, or anything? You're still in contact?'

Between their two heads a clump of trees rises out of the darkness, floodlit for a moment. Paul turns the wheel and they are gone. 'I don't know. I'm sorry. I really don't know.'

'Does he write?'

'He *has* written.'

'And do you write back?'

'Not yet.'

She says gently, 'I liked him a lot, Sarah. I liked you both.'

The hot mass under my ribs has risen higher. I can taste it now in my throat. I wonder if I am going to throw up. 'I *will* write to him,' I tell her. The tears are pricking now, at the back of my eyes. 'I'm going to write to him. One of these days, when I've got something to say.'

*

Next morning the light wakes me. I lie under the covers for a moment, waiting for messages from the outposts of my body. Nothing. Only the muffled cawing of a solitary rook, somewhere over the fields, sunlight at the corners of the curtain. The window is closed now. I pull on a sweater over my pyjamas and wander down into the kitchen, crumbs sticking to the soles of my bare feet. The tiles are like ice. I pull my old plimsolls out from where I left them, under the table. I take a jar of grapefruit juice out of the fridge. I grind coffee, my eyes vacantly scanning the grass outside. Sun streams almost horizontally through the black lace of trees in the lane. It reaches almost to the kitchen table, almost as far as my hands on either side of the china bowl. Inside me somewhere the baby suddenly flips over and flips again, like a displaced heartbeat. I feel inside my clothes for the place where the movement is, but I can't register anything yet from the outside. She is there, though, unmistakable. And last night was a dream. She is there, somersaulting tirelessly through her own element. The sun plays on the taps, on the water in the plastic washing-up bowl, casting ripples of light across the ceiling. Nothing can be very wrong with the world.

When I drive to the *Fac*, the verges of the roads are still white under a dusting of snow so thin it could be only frost. On the hard surface it has melted already, but something white still clings to the grass. I have an easy group this morning, first-years, English their second foreign language. The North African girl with the lovely eyes. I try to remember what I have planned to do with them. Some little creative thing. I make my way along the corridor, towards the departmental staffroom.

At first I think the room is empty. Then I see Laurence. She is sitting at a table in the corner by the window, her head bent over a book. I edge my way past to where the photocopies lie waiting in neat stacks. 'Hello,' I say. 'Are you feeling better?'

She looks up. 'Better?'

'You weren't there last night. Dr Stillwood said you were ill.'

'Oh, no . . .' She half smiles. 'Not really.'

'But he said . . .'

'Oh, Francis probably said that, you know, for the form. I

probably have been working too hard. I can't help it. It's so absorbing. But there's nothing the matter. Really.'

'I was quite worried.' I try to make it sound like a joke. I hear myself make an odd noise, something between a cough and a laugh. 'I thought you might have some kind of . . . eating disorder,' I say.

'Eating disorder? No. The only appetites I suffer from are . . . intellectual.' She laughs too. With me, or at me? 'And as far as last night was concerned, I just couldn't be bothered. Do you think I've got time for all that? Can you see me, honestly, sitting in some little bourgeois family restaurant at Lervain's elbow: '*Oui, Monsieur. Non, Monsieur.* How wonderfully perceptive you are, *Monsieur.* And what an extraordinary way you have with . . . do tell me, what is it? Ah, chicken livers. A provocative choice . . . but intriguing! No, really, I . . .'

She catches my eye. I am shaking. I reach past her and pick up my pile of copies. I walk out of the room, straight down the corridor towards 106, then past it and on into the students' cloakroom beyond. The blood is pounding now inside my head. Or is it my whole body that's threatening to burst open? I lock myself in a cubicle and put the pile of papers down carefully, just inside the door. My eyes start to water. I raise the seat and lean over. I push my hair back and wait. 'Hold on,' I say to Hannah, under my breath. 'Hold on, just a few months longer. I promise this isn't going to hurt.'

I have been dreaming of Francis. I wake up with an odd feeling of calm. In the dream he was looking at me, his face gentler and more open than any face I have ever seen in reality. He was saying the most terrible things. 'You're no good, Sarah. Whatever you do, you won't ever manage to be good enough,' like the final judgement of a God. 'I despise you, Sarah. Surely you know that?' And his eyes grey and clear, their expression of pure scorn indistinguishable from pure kindness. He's right. I am no good. I'm despicable. I wake in sudden conviction, with a surge of something like joy. A sexual charge there, too. Despicable. My whole body shivers, the child in it belittled, shrivelled, a dead red fish.

I get out of bed and draw the curtains. Beyond the bare branches the sky is clear. It looks cold. I can hear Dominique clattering in her kitchen. Her door scrapes open and I see her cross the yard and go round to the other side of the house, banging a wooden spoon on the side of a bowl, calling. Feeding the ducks. I step back from the window. Francis is the only person who can help me now. Truth-teller, gentle assassin. From my dream I know him. I must go to him now, not in that old tentative spirit of enquiry, but to tell him something. To tell him everything. And if the dream is anything to go by, he will understand.

I get dressed. I make myself a quick cup of coffee. I put my contacts in and clean my teeth. Then I go out to my car, parked just in front of the garage, and start to scrape the frost off the windscreen with a length of broken plastic ruler. I put my key in the ignition and turn it. At first the engine grinds impotently. Then a cough. I pull the choke out further. I drive up the hill in a series of kangaroo-hops, the cold car threatening to die on me at every turn.

I drive straight to his house, as if I knew the way already. Straight there without a single hesitation. I leave my orange Dyane in the little wedge-shaped square and walk the last hundred metres to his house.

From the front there is no sign of life. The solid wood of the door to the main house is closed. And its twin, the front door to the bedroom cottage, closed too, permanently. And in between, the rusting iron backplate of the conservatory, without a chink of light.

I don't dare to knock. A quick glance up at the street windows to make sure I have not been seen. Then I turn away and into the nearest side-street, past an *alimentation* with its crates of inclined vegetables, past a bakery where the long loaves are lined up in the racks like so many soldiers. At the bottom of his garden there is a small gate.

It is padlocked, but I climb up on to the second rung and swing my leg over. I am in the orchard. The sheep are nowhere to be seen. The grass is short now, for the winter, the blades still white in the shadows with the night's heavy frost. Here and there, a brittle leaf, its serrations outlined in white.

I make my way up towards the house. The conservatory is bare and bleak now, the chipped tiles swept, the walnut tree tensing its gnarled bare branches over the glass. In the centre, what must be the bar football machine, shrouded in a faded green cloth, the handles poking out from underneath. It looks somehow touching. I tread carefully, making no sound.

The dining-room is too high for me to see in. I climb on to the rim of an old sawn-off cider-barrel full of earth. My eyes are just higher than the sill.

He is there. He is turned slightly away from me, sitting on an upholstered chaise longue under the other window. He is wearing a strange garment, a sort of light dressing-gown that has slipped sideways to show his chest. Yet there is no fire in the grate. The two bottom corners of the glass are frosted with white ferns.

He isn't reading. There isn't a single book to be seen in the room. Even the magazines and loose papers have been cleared away. There is no lute propped on the window-seat in the corner. Even the walls are quite bare.

I raise my fist to tap on the glass. Then I think better of it. But the small movement has made me lose my balance slightly. My fingers scrabble for a moment on the flaking paint of the window-sill and he turns in my direction.

He doesn't see me. He looks away again almost at once. But I have seen him. The face of my dream. Joy. Under the thin robe he is naked. And his cheeks are streaming with tears.

I let myself down quietly and go back. My car is where I left it. I brush a fragment of dead twig from the bonnet. I unlock the door and climb in. I fasten my seat-belt and go to turn the key in the ignition. But I must have knocked against the rear-view mirror as I got in. I reach up to straighten it with my right hand.

And my hand jumps back, as if burnt by its cold touch. Trapped in the curve of the glass I can see Lervain, a miniature figure in a thigh-length coat and soft scarf, bending to lock his car.

I sit quite still. He straightens up and crosses the frame to where Francis's house proffers its closed grey façade. I see him raise his fist in a silent knock.

I wait. I lower my head slightly, trying to get a view of the windows. Do I imagine an upstairs shutter moves? Lervain leans back on his heels, surveying the street, his hands in his pockets. He knocks again. This time I can almost hear him.

Then he crosses to the opposite pavement and stands there for a moment, looking up. Finally he unlocks his car again and gets in. I see him back towards the mouth of a narrow one-way street and turn down into it. His dark blue Peugeot slips into the tight opening and is gone. I wind down my window and hear him change up through the gears, into third, hooting once at some obstruction. I still listen, as the faint purr of his powerful engine gradually recedes.

5

I HAVE ASKED TO SEE LERVAIN, a formal interview, before it is too late. After hours, when there will be no one to interrupt us. I leave you lying on the bed, the book of classic screenplays open face downwards on the floor beside you, where it has fallen, Berlioz filling the narrow rooms with that fierce lament. I glance once at you before leaving. Your eyes are closed. I can't tell whether or not you are asleep.

I turn out the light. On the bed you don't move. I tiptoe out to the kitchen and then on to the dark landing. I close the door of our flat behind me with a little click.

I drive to the outskirts, to where the dirty whitish buildings of the university squat on their familiar piece of ground, the dusty trees already almost stripped by the autumn storms. I climb the echoing stairway to the usual corridor. I pass 101, 106, 107.

I am feeling sick again. These days it is quite bad. In the evenings, particularly, when my stomach is empty. *Morning sickness.* I catch myself smiling at the irony. Yet I don't feel much like eating. I can't look at a cup of coffee. It has been all I could do to hide it from everyone. With you I have cooked up excuses – a headache, a bug, a hangover. Something not as fresh as it should be. And you don't seem to have noticed anything out of the ordinary, talking and laughing as usual, reading your books and listening to your tapes as I close the bathroom door on myself each night at about this time and vomit into the toilet, my noise drowned out by the homeward procession of traffic outside. Every evening I slowly recover. We eat the meal I have somehow managed to cook. Your face comes alive as you tell me about your work. You feel free here, suddenly. It's exciting. Something important is suddenly happening to you in this foreign place.

I glance at my watch. About three minutes to six. It is almost dark outside already. I turn the handle of the staffroom door and go in.

127

Lervain is there, waiting for me. He is sitting at the table under the window, the densely printed pages of a periodical open in front of him, his face almost greenish in the harsh overhead fluorescent lighting. 'Ah,' he says. 'You wanted to see me. Do come in.'

'Thank you.' I take off my jacket and hang it on the door. 'It was kind of you to give up the time.'

'Not at all. We pride ourselves on looking after our foreign visitors. But . . .' He smiles and waves his hand. 'You're hardly that, now. Over a year since you first came. I can hardly believe it. You're almost one of us.'

'Thank you,' I say again.

He points to a chair opposite him and I sit down. He leans forward, over the printed pages, one elbow resting on the paper. It crinkles slightly under the pressure. 'So. Is the term starting well? What can I do for you?'

'It's starting very well.' Apart from feeling shagged out and sick all the time. 'In fact . . .'

'Yes?'

'I was wondering if there might be any chance of a further extension.'

He pulls back from me, sitting up straighter in his chair. 'You surprise me, Mademoiselle. It's rather soon, surely? The new school year's barely started.'

'I know. But for my own sake . . . I wondered.'

He looks down at his cuffs. He clasps his hands together over the desk, opening and closing his fingers. On the tightly printed page the shadow-wings open and close. 'Is there any reason for this sudden . . . whim?'

'I love what I'm doing.'

He looks at me. 'I know you do.'

'And I want to stay here.' I swallow hard and the nausea recedes slightly. 'To be absolutely honest, there's nothing for me at home.'

For a long time he says nothing. He stands up and goes to the door. He rummages in his coat pocket and comes back with a packet of cigarettes and a lighter. A little silver lighter with something engraved on it, something I can't read. He flips it open and sucks the cigarette into life. 'You're not thinking of getting married, are you?'

'No.'

He takes a long drag and lets the smoke out slowly. It surrounds me like a fog. For a moment I can't even see him properly. My stomach heaves. 'Because I can quite see what that would do for your career prospects in England. They don't make any secret of that.'

'I'm not thinking of getting married,' I tell him.

He looks at me shrewdly. 'You'll have had your two years.'

'I know.'

'And the new woman – what's her name? – the one with the child – she may want to stay on, and in that case . . .'

'I know,' I say again. I could snatch the Gauloise from his hand and grind it out on the polished wood of the desk. 'I just thought there might be something . . .'

He shrugs. 'I'll keep my ear to the ground, of course. You never know. Sometimes things do come up. At a higher level, though, usually. I shouldn't bank on anything, if I were you. I wouldn't be honest if I pretended . . .'

I wait for him to finish, but he doesn't. He takes a last drag from the cigarette and stubs it out in the glass ashtray. Pastis 51. I try one last time. 'I do genuinely think I could be useful.'

Something in his face changes, setting into a fixed expression of what is meant to pass for kindness. Somewhere behind his eyes something closes. 'Oh yes. Certainly. I'm not denying that.'

My voice almost cracks now, with the effort. 'I've worked hard this past year. Have you even seen what I've . . . ?'

He gets up and pats me on the shoulder. Fatherly, almost. He takes down his raincoat from the peg on the door, picks up his briefcase. 'Mademoiselle . . .'

I look at him, willing him to leave.

'You'd do better to go home,' he says. 'There's no future here, for foreigners. Even in languages. Even if you can get another year, then what? You have to go back eventually. You can't ever really be one of us. You'd have to take the *Aggrég.*, change your nationality . . . Ask Francis.'

My voice is shaking now, unmistakably. 'Thank you. I will.'

'By the way . . .' he says.

'Yes?'

'I put something in your pigeon-hole. It's an invitation.

Every year the *Rectorat* invites one of us to its champagne Reception, at the beginning of December. *Pâté de foie gras*, a little man in livery who calls out your name as you come down the stairs – you'll enjoy it.'

'Thank you,' I say again.

'*De rien.*' For a fraction of a second I catch the trace of a southern accent, a different, fictitious, Lervain in a different, Mediterranean setting. 'We always send someone. Two people, in fact. One member of the teaching staff, and one student. It's an experience. You'll see.'

'Yes.'

He opens the door and stands on the threshold for a moment, hesitating. 'And, Sarah . . .' he says.

'*Monsieur*?'

'Don't get married.' He doesn't give me time to answer. In the space of a moment his folded raincoat is swallowed by the crack of the door.

One Sunday we drive out of the city – up through Bayeux and then northwest towards the coast. It is late October. The ragged landscape passes us in a smell of wet – a flock of crows in a field, the dark mass of a forest with mist still caught between the trees. As we get nearer, the taste of salt in the mist, grey air pulled straight inland from the surface of the Channel. The tide is out, the wide stretch of beach half invisible, apparently deserted. In spite of the cold, we take off our shoes.

We walk along the edge of the waves, laughing and screaming when the creeping water suddenly catches us, swirling round our ankles. Now and again we stop to pick up stones or shells at the tideline. Once you chase me with a heavy flag of seaweed that flaps against my face with a crack like wet cloth, and leaves me covered with tracks of salt. I fill my pockets with pebbles, a piece of driftwood that is like part of a grey skeleton, a section of collar-bone or pelvis broken and polished by sea. Where the path begins, you bend down to kiss me. 'I love you,' you say, as we start to climb.

The thing looms over us like a visitor from an alien planet, or a grim totem. We are shivering, our wet hands red in the cold wind. Your teeth are chattering as you read it: 'The allied forces landing on this shore . . .' Your American voice rises at the end of each breath-group. You could be reading poetry, or asking a question. 'Did I ever tell you about my uncle?' you say.

We stand in that half-moon of garden, with its 1557 names of the missing, the paths radiating from the centre like wheel-spokes. We aren't laughing. We aren't smiling, even. I am thinking of the dead, of your young uncle, of the cells frantically multiplying inside me in a small tangle, the translucent red threads clinging to the walls.

And by November you have gone. One morning, quite suddenly, you decide to leave. You buy a plane ticket. You fill cardboard boxes with books and tapes and papers and send them to yourself by surface mail. You fill your two suitcases and the one rucksack with clothes.

And once you have gone, our little flat is uninhabitable. The rustling tissue paper that covers the chimney wakes me in the night and I lie there crying. I can't be bothered to cook for myself. The chipped saucepans stay clean on their rack. Until one morning I finally admit it: this is no way to live. I close my eyes for a moment and my whole existence is filled with the buzz of passing mopeds. I try to imagine how it will be, once I have the child.

But I am lucky. Somehow on the grapevine I hear of a cottage, twenty kilometres or so to the south-west, empty. I drive out one afternoon to see it, my heart thumping. I take it all in – the stone-tiled kitchen with its stained benches and open shelving behind rough curtains. The sofa and white wicker chairs, the woodstove. Outside, the turning autumn trees, cows grazing on the far bank of a pond. And upstairs, that big light attic bedroom, the space under the slope of the low ceiling where I shall be able to put the cot.

It takes me two trips to ferry my belongings from the city. The landlady helps me, slightly inquisitive and over-friendly, but well intentioned. She takes one end of my big metal trunk, and together we carry it up to the landing. '*Je vous remercie, Madame.*' I rub my hands on the sides of my jeans, leaving a streak of rust.

'Call me Dominique,' she says.

'I'm Sarah.'

We go down to the kitchen. She nods to me and lets herself out. As she crosses the gravel towards her own front door she calls back to me, 'Let me know if you want a hand with anything else.' I see her disappear between the plants that frame her kitchen doorway, their buds already blackened by frost. I hear her door close.

And then I am on my own.

That night.

I go over it again and again, how you stood in the doorway. How even as you came in you seemed suddenly to sense something, as if you could still go back, as if you could still turn on your heels and get out of that flat before anything definitive was said.

How you said, 'What is it? What's wrong with you?' How the evening procession of mopeds seemed to have gone suddenly quiet, how even the water seemed to go still in the radiators. Only the soup I was stirring still bubbled in its chipped pan.

How you sat down at the plastic-topped table, rubbed a spot of wet from your sleeve, looked at me. 'What is it? What's wrong? Do you have a headache? Are you sick or something?' How I didn't pass the back of my hand across my forehead and faint gracefully at your feet.

I said, 'My period didn't come. And I keep feeling sick.'

'What?'

I didn't repeat it. You weren't asking me to repeat it. How you got up and just walked into the bedroom and shut the door quietly behind you. How I turned off the gas and watched the soup as the bubbles gradually subsided, a skin slowly forming on the surface, something brownish and glutinous that wrinkled when I tried to move the wooden spoon.

I am so tired. I sit down on the stairs and lean my head against the banisters, looking down between them into the piles of bags and boxes that still almost cover the sitting-room rug. In a minute I shall have to go down and sort through them, take the kitchen things into the kitchen, the upstairs things up to the bedroom to be put away.

On my own. For a moment I see you clearly, feel the

slippery geography of your mouth. 'I love you,' I had said when you first kissed me. Not the way you said it to me at the beach, but something else, jumping the mind's barriers cleanly into darkness.

But I shall always disappoint you. Because it is the lost dialects of intimacy itself I find erotic. A very female view, no doubt. And now I shall disappoint you even more, because of the child.

I ache all over. It must be from carrying the boxes. That heavy trunk. I grip the banisters with my hands and watch the blood drain from my knuckles. I stretch my legs as far as they will go across the bare wood treads of the stairs.

My right foot knocks against something. I hear it slither away from me across the smooth surface and fall to the next step with a sharp crack. When I stand up, I accidentally kick it again with my toe and it goes crashing down to the living-room floor. I go to the bottom and pick it up.

It is your tape, the one you were always listening to. You must have forgotten to pack it with the others. I put my thumbnail into the toothed centre of one of the spools and twist until a loop of narrow ribbon protrudes. There is a pair of scissors in the bag of kitchen stuff, on the rug just in front of the stove.

I go back up and sit on the stairs again, higher this time, almost at the top. I pull the dark loop steadily until the whole thing unravels, its tangle of black entrails glistening in my lap. Then I take the scissors and cut it into little flakes, focusing my whole mind on the neat scraps as I haven't concentrated on anything since childhood, as I can't imagine concentrating on anything ever again. My lap is full of black stuff. When I stand up and shake my clothes, the whole pile falls around me, darkening the treads of the stairs, glittering as it falls between the banisters to the sitting-room below, so much inaudible French singing, so much black confetti turning in the air, settling on the start of my new life.

When I go in to the university the next morning, something is not quite right. On the steps outside the students are gathered in small groups, talking earnestly, shifting from one foot to the other in the cold wind, smoking, crushing the dead butts under their feet. I push past them to the glass doors. The big bare foyer is almost empty. Torn posters advertise political meetings and cultural events, fluttering in the draught from the door. Some of them happened months ago. I barely glance at them as I cross the echoing hall and make for the stairs.

The English corridor is oddly silent. Some of the classroom doors are open. I glimpse a few students, standing, or sitting on desks, hardly talking. The corridor itself is empty.

When I open the door of the staffroom I draw in my breath. The room is half full – I catch sight of Paul, Mireille, Lervain, Helen and a couple of the other *lecteurs* over by the window. Everyone is uncharacteristically serious. Some of them are looking almost guilty, as if I have caught them in the middle of some misdemeanour, some verbal blunder bitten off mid-syllable. Mireille sees me and threads her way between them to where I am standing. She takes my hand.

'What is it?' It comes out as something hardly louder than a whisper. Around me the voices have sprung up again in a low murmur. I strain to make out the words.

'Sarah . . .' Her eyes fill with tears.

My first thought is that it is something to do with you. You are trapped or injured, the victim of some natural disaster. Suddenly I need to sit down. 'What is it? Why's everyone here? What's happened?'

'Sarah, it's Francis.' She is clutching my hand with a kind of urgency, her fingers closed on mine so tightly I can hardly feel my own. 'He took sleeping-pills. Friday night, probably. No one knew anything about it until this morning. His *femme de ménage . . .'*

I breathe. I wait for the room to stop rocking, for the voices to stop splintering around me. 'It's not possible.'

'I'm afraid it's the truth.'

I stumble out and back down the corridor to 106. It is half empty. There are perhaps five students to hear me and look up. Mouna, the little Algerian girl, is crying openly, her face buried in her arms, her shoulders shaking. 'No class today,' I tell them. 'I'll see you all next week.' They nod at me, without speaking. I realise my own eyes are running over. I can't help it. Head down, I leave the room and make quickly for the stairs.

I sit looking at the crusted black glass of the woodstove. It is not possible. He was the one person who could help me, who could have explained something. In my mind he had become almost a myth. And myths don't die. He has to go on.

I jump at a light tap on the window. I get up and unlock the door, my fingers stiff with the damp cold. At first I can't see anyone. Then I make out an elderly man, bent over something. My eyes adjust to the darkness and I recognise Robert, Dominique's husband. 'I hope I'm not disturbing you. It's such a rotten night. I thought I could give you a demonstration.'

'I'm sorry, I don't quite . . .' I say.

'The woodstove.'

'Oh. Yes. How kind of you.' I stand back to let him pass. He comes in like a hunchback, doubled up over a pile of logs, kindling, newspaper. He grunts as he lets it go. The logs fall out of his arms and roll across the stones of the hearth.

He kneels in front of the open glass door, making tight balls of newspaper, snapping off twigs until they are the right length. Then the logs. He rubs the moss and bark from his fingers. 'That's all it is. That's all you have to do. Then just set a match to it, when you're ready. Keep the damper open until it gets really hot. Then you'll find you can close it up a bit. It's rather temperamental sometimes, if the wind's in the wrong place. You'll see.'

'I'm so grateful.'

He only grunts again. 'If you have any problems, just give us a shout.'

'Thank you. I will.'

'We're only next door. My wife will have told you.'

'Yes.'

He reaches for the matches on the stone mantelpiece and throws them across to me as he goes to the door. The big box lands in my lap.

At first the thing goes like a dream. The flames from the rolled-up paper lick the kindling into life. The kindling cracks and spits. The iron chamber ticks steadily as it expands. Then there is a lull. The flames on the logs sink lower, flicker desultorily and go out one by one. I open the glass door to give it more air, and my sitting-room begins to fill with billowing black smoke.

I open the outside doors to let it clear. The cottage is as cold as ever now. But little by little the flames pick up. The black iron starts to tick again. The muffled roar in the black pipe gets louder. And finally the whole metal box is lit up in red, the long tongues curling like water over the fire-bricks, searing the charred deposits from the inside of the glass.

I can't believe that Francis is dead. It is quite simply impossible. I feel a sudden desperate need to make time go backwards, to turn back the clock and let him be alive again. I'm the one who has to make him go on. I have to make him do what I need him to do – be kind to me, or hurt me exactly as I would wish to be hurt. I have to make him tell me what he knows.

But the spirit has gone out of it, somehow. From now on, whatever he does will never be quite convincing. Nothing I can say or do will redeem him, or ourselves as we were when we first met. Dead, he is beyond redemption. I must have loved him, I realise. Not as I love you, but a kind of love nevertheless. And he took that small bottle of pills in his own hands. He swallowed his own future, and part of ours.

But there is Hannah, a sudden small crick of life almost as long as my little finger. It is time to let the dead people die. The heat from the open stove scalds my face, lights up my hands in a flicker of orange. I am getting warm at last. I stretch my body out gratefully, full length on the rug.

It seems to me that every day now I feel a little more pregnant, that every day, when I look at myself in the tarnished mirror of the old *armoire* in the bedroom, something has changed. Not that I have put on any weight yet. If anything I am thinner – the sickness is keeping me thin. But my breasts have grown tighter and heavier. I can see the veins in them more clearly, the way they meet and divide under the skin like blue rivers, the small tributaries every day more numerous. And my nipples surrounded by small red pimples, so that it is difficult to tell where the ordinary skin ends and the areola begins, the whole area sensitive to the touch, slightly painful.

I tell myself about the baby, I try to visualise a tiny red fish-like thing growing inside me in darkness, I tell myself this is what it feels like, a new life beginning. But it feels more like a death. Every evening the same sickness, the same irretrievable separation from you. I tell myself that I am getting closer, closer to the moment when I shall see the child, when I shall finally know whether she is to look like you, or like me, or like neither of us so much as herself.

And my classes continue. No one knows about the baby. No one seems to suspect, even. Most of the time I hurry from car-park to staffroom to classroom, avoiding all eye contact. It isn't the baby that disturbs me, so much as the fear that someone might start talking to me about Francis. Or about you.

The end of November. After that last fierce wind two nights ago, the trees are virtually bare – only the odd obstinate leaf still clinging here and there in the lower branches. And at last the sickness is receding. Buildings no longer rock almost imperceptibly under me as if becalmed and floating. The earth feels almost solid under my feet.

The *maîtrise* group are there in force: only Laurence is missing. Marthe sits in her usual corner, hunched over her notes as if she hasn't noticed me come in. I catch the others glancing at her slyly. They look back at me and grin. Jean-Luc raises his eyebrows. Eight weeks into the new term, and already we know one another. Already the little allegiances have sprung up, the identity of the adversary is clear.

I try to cut through it. I open my file with a snap. When she glances up I am looking in her direction. 'Well. Your proses,' I say to her. 'How shall we do it this week?'

There is a moment of silence. Then she says, 'We could do what we used to do with M. Lervain last year.'

'What did you do?'

'We took one prose out of the pile and used that as our starting point. We corrected it, as a class, if you like.'

'Oh, *no*.' Serge groans. 'I used to hate that. He always seemed to pick on mine.'

'How did he choose whose work to look at?' I ask her.

'Just like that. It was random, I think.' She sits there with

137

her arms folded. She looks round the class, meeting every-one's eyes. It is a kind of challenge.

'All right.' I take the sheaf of papers and go over to where she is. I turn the pile upside down and hold it out to her, fanned out, as if I were asking her to take an unseen card. 'You choose. Just take one.'

She feels in the pile and pulls out a double copy from the centre. Pale blue squared paper. Neat handwriting, done with a fountain-pen and proper ink. 'Laurence Chaulieux,' I say. 'She's not here. Try again.'

Marthe lifts her head. 'Does it matter?'

'I'm sorry?'

'Why should it matter that she isn't here?'

'She's not well,' Jean-Luc says. 'She hasn't been well, ever since . . .'

'You can hardly criticise her work when she's not here to defend herself.' Serge brings his fist down on the desk with a thud. Papers fly off on to the floor and he leans to retrieve them.

Marthe looks at me. 'I don't see why not.' She runs her hand through her short hair and half smiles. 'It's quite an impersonal exercise. It's the language itself we're interested in, surely? She wouldn't want us to make special allowances for her. That's patronising. I really don't see why we shouldn't.'

'Okay,' I say slowly.

At the back of the class someone gives a nervous laugh. I go back to the front and spread Laurence's copy on the teacher's desk. 'Find the original, then,' I tell them. I wait for them all to rummage in their files and briefcases. When they look up again, I start to read.

I read out the first sentence, trying to say the English naturally, trying not to give them any clues. 'Is that perfect?' I ask them. 'Can anyone improve on that, or is that the best we can do?'

There is a silence. Then Denise says, tentatively, 'I think "pejorative" isn't very English, somehow.'

'You're right. It's not wrong. But it's not as idiomatic as it could be. And in this whole, rather contemporary context . . .'

'It's a bit literary,' Jean-Luc puts in.

'So? What do you suggest? Marthe?'

' "Disparaging"? "Derogatory"?'

' "Derogatory",' Jean-Luc calls out.

I go to the blackboard and start to write. 'Let's put them both in, for the time being,' I say. 'We can do the fine tuning at the end.' I turn round to face them again. 'Anything else?'

'Oh, no. It's perfect otherwise.' Marthe is looking straight at me as she says it, watching my face. 'Beyond reproach.'

I feel myself start to frown. Is she being sarcastic? Or is that what she really thinks? Laurence's first sentence still rings in my head, as much a part of Laurence as her voice and as foreign, full of an unidiomatic music that is nevertheless a kind of grace. I put the stub of chalk on the desk and rub my hands. I sit down.

'You're talking complete rubbish,' someone says from the back, right on cue. 'It's completely un-English. It's useless.'

'*Ouais*,' Jean-Luc says.

'Any *1er D.E.U.G.* could do better. It's absolute shit.'

'So?' I say calmly. 'Give us your version. Would you like to tell us what you think it *should* be?'

And it is then that I begin to see that it is getting out of control, the class splitting almost cleanly into two bitter camps and Laurence at the centre, a mangled shred of herself. For nearly an hour the argument rages until finally they retreat, exhausted. Marthe herself hardly contributes anything. She is looking down as usual, writing notes to herself in the margins. I catch her eye only once. Exultant. Yes. And well she should be. I am the one responsible, the one who has let it happen. It is my own fatuous kindness that has betrayed them all.

When I get home I go straight upstairs and lie down on the bed. The woodstove is unlit, and the cottage is cold. I am shivering. It is so cold in the bedroom I can see my breath. I pull the blankets up to my chin and lie there looking at the ceiling, feeling the covers across my body like a heavy weight. From time to time I doze off, my half-sleep full of Marthe and Jean-Luc and Laurence, gesticulating wildly, chasing me through the dark streets as I try to escape them, my arms full of dressing-up clothes – fringed skirts and red lace long-Johns, a silver lurex bustier, a floppy black hat with a crushed velvet rose. I shall never teach them again. And you. Over and over again you are leaving me. You are standing in that doorway. 'What is it?' you're saying. 'What's wrong?' You shut the bedroom door behind you, and I am alone in our little kitchen, my hand on the gas-tap. The flame under the chipped saucepan sinks to a small blue constellation, then pops as the jets go out. In the pan the bubbles gradually subside, as a thick brown skin forms round the bowl of the wooden spoon, wrinkling when I try to stir. Faces in it, a glaze of something that could be tears. Over and over again, Francis empties the bottle of sleeping-pills into his left hand.

After a while I wake. I need to empty my bladder. I walk across the bare boards of the landing, my toes curling up against the cold. I go into the bathroom, pull down my knickers, prepare to lower myself on to the seat. And then I see it. In the middle of the gusset there is a pale pink spot of something that seems to be blood.

Hannah. She is trying to communicate with me, in the only language she knows. I pull on a coat and drag myself downstairs. I let myself out and stumble the few steps to Dominique's kitchen door. I knock on it, as loudly as I dare.

At first they don't hear me. Their two voices rise and fall, comforting, punctuated by laughter. Dominique's sandpaper contralto, and Robert's grumbling bass. I knock again, louder. I hear the scrape of a chair on stone, quick footsteps. Dominique opens the door and sees me standing there on the top step.

'Sarah! Come in.' I must look dreadful, my hair tousled, the old coat pulled close over crumpled clothes.

'Can I use your phone?'

'Of course you can.'

She takes me through to the hall. She retreats and closes the door behind me discreetly. I hear them resume their quiet conversation, muffled by old wood. I lift the receiver and dial Lervain's home number.

'*Allô?*' I recognise his clipped voice.

'Hello? It's Sarah,' I say. 'I just wanted to warn you.' It is the wrong word. 'I mean . . .'

'*Oui?*'

'I wanted to let you know I won't be in tomorrow. Perhaps not for a day or two. I'm so sorry.'

'Are you ill?'

'Yes.' I cough. I try to speak through my nose. 'It could be flu, I think.'

'*Pauvre petite.*' I can't tell whether or not it is ironic. '*Reposez-vous.* I hope you feel better soon.'

Thank you. I will. A couple of days . . .'

'No hurry,' he says easily. 'I'll get one of the *lecteurs* to cover your classes. Helen, possibly.'

'Thank you. You're very understanding.'

He makes deprecatory noises. I murmur a last excuse and put the phone down on its rest.

I go back into the kitchen. Dominique comes over to me and puts her arm round my shoulders. 'Are you all right?'

'Why shouldn't I be all right?'

'You look as if you've seen a ghost.'

'I was only talking to my Head of Department.'

'Is he . . . intimidating?'

'Not specially.'

'Aagh!' She makes that odd sound in her throat. 'Would you like a cup of tea? Or something stronger?'

'No. Thank you. I must get back.'

'Are you keeping warm over there?'

'Yes. Thank you.'

'There's that little electric radiator up in the bedroom. Don't be shy about using it. And don't work so hard.' She stands back to survey me critically. 'You're looking tired.'

'I am tired. But I'm going to have a quiet week. I won't be doing so much from now on.'

I stay in bed, then. I hardly get up. I lie under the covers reading, or listening to the little transistor radio, or just thinking. Sometimes I sleep. I listen to the noises the cottage makes, the low roar of the wind in the trees outside, the squawk of some unidentified bird. I lie as still as I can, turning over only when my spine starts to ache or one of my limbs has started to go numb. Even asleep I am aware of the stillness of my body. I get up only to make myself a sandwich or pour a glass of milk or orange juice, or to go to the bathroom.

And when I go to the bathroom, it is always the same, the pad between my legs still spotted faintly pink in the centre.

Or brownish. Once, a clear, bright red that makes my hand shake as I change it. And then a pattern of tiny wet threads, like fern-fronds, or red lace.

The days merge into one another. I listen to *France Musique*, distorted by the vagaries of the weather. I hear Schubert, Bach, a hauntingly lovely soprano and flute piece by someone whose name I don't catch. Once, the *Symphonie fantastique*, in a brief interval of calm – music and weather fusing in a single ambiguous message. Once it is Brahms, a tricky unpredictable sequence for clarinet and piano that seems to take me to where the child is waiting, her fine hair haloed in sun. She runs from me across wet sand, in a brief white flash. Outside, thunder. And then it is actually snowing, a slither of melting white stuff that makes its crooked way down the pane to collect at the bottom of the glass.

And in spite of everything I am feeling more myself. Less sick. Less sleepy. I wake at night tingling with suppressed excitement. Something is going to happen. One of these days you will come back to me. You will arrive unexpectedly. You will have flown here for a death, or a wedding. Francis and Laurence, her veil thrown off as she steps out into the open. Our hands will find each other, as we stand shoulder to shoulder, somewhere at the back.

Francis. His books and manuscripts shipped back to baffled, loving parents in England. His exotic sheep sold, the grass in the orchard growing unchecked. The gnarled branches of the walnut pruned to obscene stumps, and the conservatory glass in fragments, smashed by kids from the village. I imagine it glittering on the tiles, on the shrouded bar football machine, collecting in the folds of the green cloth.

And you are three thousand miles away, in Boston. Where you are the new day is only just beginning. Here the sun has almost reached its winter zenith, filtered obliquely through bare branches to make a waving pattern on the far wall. I can see myself in the big dark mirror of the *armoire*, my face still pale over the covers. I throw them off and kneel up on the bed. I take off my pyjamas and stare at myself, a naked praying figure in an almost empty room.

I start to touch myself. Slowly, at first, my finger hardly moving, waiting for the mind to precede it with visions, attentive to the small slow architecture of the dream. My pregnant body is so lovely – the skin taut over my heavy breasts, the red stretch-marks starting to glow across them like scratches. The curve of my belly just beginning. Or am I imagining it? Surely my waist is starting to thicken already? I see myself reflected in the mirror, partly in shadow, swaying, my face stupid with absence. No mind. No language. And as my finger moves faster, my other hand straying over my chest, my face, my thighs, my mouth, there can be no doubt of it. I close my eyes. And somewhere at the edges of the darkness, Francis is not dead. You are certain to come back to me. Inside me, in that most intimate of all possible places, our first child is waiting to be born.

I am standing at the top of a marble staircase. Ahead of me, the wide descending sweep that leads down into that moving throng of people. I am wearing my slate-blue silk dress. I have to remind myself not to pinch and crease the fabric between my fingers. A liveried official stoops to catch my name.

And then I am descending. Only one or two hear the announcement and look up, an expression of mild puzzlement on their faces, but I feel myself redden. It is difficult to take the last few steps without stumbling or losing my balance.

The big room glitters with the light of several chandeliers. Huge arrangements of expensive flowers on every table – lilies and irises and long-stemmed roses, feathery greenery that casts delicate shadows on the white linen cloths. Great oval platters of canapés – *bouchées de langoustine*, little squares of *pâté de foie gras* with their small dark chips of truffle embedded in the pinkish-grey mousse, asparagus tips like green spearheads pointing in alternate directions, interlocking like sardines. And everywhere the glossy-coated waiters, their salvers of glasses held up at shoulder-level as they negotiate the surge of bodies. The fragile flutes with their steady stream of rising bubbles. I pick one from a tray as it goes past.

I sip it and question my body, as if rolling my tongue round the base of an intermittently aching tooth. If I concentrate hard I can just feel the steady slow seepage. But it is nothing. No better, but no worse. Certainly not a distress-call. Barely even a shy greeting. It is even slightly comforting, a tangible sign that she is still there inside me, still part of me, and alive.

'Do you work in the field of education?'

I jump. There is a man at my elbow, slightly elderly. He is biting into a vol-au-vent. The small crumbs of puff pastry hang in his moustache. 'Yes. I teach, actually.'

'School?'

'University.'

'And you're not from this part of France.'

'I'm not from France at all, in fact. I'm English.'

'You're English?'

'Completely.'

'You surprise me.'

I am blushing. 'Well . . . I've been coming to France since I was quite young. They say that helps.'

'But you speak so well! I wouldn't have guessed you were English!'

'Oh . . .' He is wearing brown shoes, oddly touching with the grey suit, its sharp creases. 'The accent's okay, mostly. But I get tongue-tied. Especially when I'm feeling embarrassed. People often take me for a Frenchwoman with a severe communication difficulty!'

His eyes twinkle at me. 'And is that better than being English? Here, have you tried one of these?' He picks up the great tray and holds it under my nose. 'They're very good.'

'Thank you.' I bite into it. He's right. I lean over to the table and take a folded napkin from the pile. 'And what do you do?'

'Oh, I'm . . . in administration.' He shrugs. 'I work here. Not for much longer.'

'You're just coming up for retirement?'

'In fifteen weeks.'

I look up at him through my fringe. 'And how many days?'

'Ah . . .' He waves his hand. 'You've seen right through me, Mademoiselle.' He is laughing. 'Two days, four hours, and fifty-five minutes precisely. But . . .' He lowers his voice. 'I love my job. I always have.'

'Yes.'

'And when the fifty-five minutes are up . . .'

It's my turn to smile.

'I'll be very sad, I assure you.'

'And then?'

'And then . . . I'll leave this country. Something I've wanted to do for a long time. *Also.*'

'Where will you go?' I am drinking fast now. A waiter passes us and my companion takes two full glasses from his tray.

'England.'

'Really?'

'Why not? I've always loved your country. We bought a house there a couple of years ago, my wife and I. Devon. It's very . . . picturesque. Unspoiled, I think you'd call it.'

'That's very brave.' Already my new glass is almost empty. 'Do you speak the language, both of you?'

'Well . . .' he says. 'After hearing you, I'm not sure how I ought to answer that.'

'You could try "Yes".'

He smiles at me and raises his glass. 'Yes, then.' For a moment I have the bizarre impression that he is going to kiss me on the mouth.

I move away from him discreetly. I glance back over my shoulder and see that he is talking to someone else, another man. He laughs and claps the stranger on the shoulder. For a moment I stand alone at one of the long tables, in a few square centimetres of space. I try the *pâté de foie gras*. I try one of the little biscuits piled with caviare. At the end of the table is an almost empty tray, one or two full glasses still unclaimed, the bubbles rising more slowly now. I slip my empty glass in beside them on the white lace doiley and take another full one in its place. Just behind me a low voice says, '*Cheers!*'

I turn round. It is Marthe, in an Indian skirt and a patchwork waistcoat over what seems to be a T-shirt. I feel the tears pricking behind my eyes. I take a deep breath. But the room is starting to turn around me, the overdressed people are like dancers meeting and parting in an odd frenetic Viennese waltz, the men's scalps shining in the crystal glare, the women's make-up smeared with motion. 'I'm not sure we've got anything to say to each other.'

'No. Didn't I ever tell you? I hate foreigners.' She laughs. But she is not laughing. In this room of steadily drinking people she may be the only person who is completely sober, completely in charge of herself. Very deliberately, she raises her hand and touches my cheek.

And I am shaking. For some time, I realise, I have been shaking. The sweat breaks out across my skin. Has she seen it? Am I going to throw up? But no. Not yet, anyway. I am quite simply in pain, a long contraction that runs through me like a deep tremor, bypassing the normal channels of recognition, translating itself directly into nausea and expending itself in a sick shudder. Not in pain. Ill. My teeth are chattering. 'Marthe, I'm not well,' I say. 'I don't think I can manage to drive. Can you please take me home?'

Somehow I make it to her car. The strap of my handbag slides from my shoulder and the bag itself falls to the metal floor at my feet. I kick it into the corner. The wide streets and public buildings of the city centre give way to a narrower maze of older façades. There is nothing here I recognise. Once, the bone-shaking clatter of cobbles, shocking as an unseen cattle-grid. My body clenches against it. Once, a big church rises out of the darkness, floodlit at the head of its short flight of steps. I blink and I can still see photographs, mounted on their accordion of screens. This is all a dream, something that happened thirty or forty years ago. In there in the darkness an old man in a cap picks his way over the stones, his face gaunt and unshaven, his eyes hidden, unreadable. A woman with a hat stands holding the hands of her two children, her astrakhan collar almost indistinguishable from the curls of her dark hair. The little girls stare out into the empty nave, wide-eyed against a background of smoke. Then the noise and glare fall away behind us. We are out of the city now, streaking between dark fields and forests of tall pines, our white path narrowing in front of us, a tunnel of projected light.

Marthe drives in on to the patch of flat gravel between the garage-barn and the house. At Dominique's end, the ground-floor windows make a yellow splash across the grass. My cottage is in darkness. Marthe comes round and opens the door on my side. For a moment she stands there uncertainly, wondering if she should help me out. But I am managing. She watches me swing my legs across the sill and stand up gingerly. 'Key?' she says.

146

I have been clutching it in my hand since that first moment, the instant I first knew I would have to leave. It is as warm as my body. It sticks slightly to my palm. I concentrate on holding it steady as it slips sideways across the metal surround, missing the hole in the dark.

'Here. Let me.' She takes it from me and the door opens smoothly. She flicks a switch and the kitchen blinks into existence, my lunch dishes still unwashed in the sink. The strip-light buzzes for a moment, a disembodied swarm of insects, futuristic. Then it goes quiet. 'Are you sure you'll be all right on your own?'

I hear the loud cough of her starter, the odd creaking purr as she puts the car into reverse. First, second, third. Second again, for the steep hill. Quieter now, as the engine recedes. Almost impossible to hear her as she stops at the top to look both ways. Then a final muted burst as she turns out into the main road, fading rapidly. And then nothing. An owl, somewhere close by in the trees. I go to the bathroom to change the pad I am wearing. It is soaked with blood. A clot of something, like a black grape. I steady myself against the wall as I change it. Somehow I clean my teeth and get into my pyjamas. I put an empty plastic bowl by the bed and slide in between the covers. The room is so dark I can hardly even make out the lighter square of the window.

I can't stop shivering. My jaw vibrates, making my teeth rattle. A wave of something radiates from somewhere low down, tightening every muscle in my body in an involuntary spasm. 'Relax,' I tell myself. 'Breathe.' I lean out over the edge of the bed and retch into the bowl.

I lie back on the pillow, too dizzy even to get up for a drink of water. The edges of the darkness push in on me, open out, push in again, swarming with points of colour – crimson, red, orange – massing and swirling, teased out fast-forward across the reeling geography of my room like a drunken sunset. Only the faint pale square of the window still holds steady. Then even that starts to vibrate slightly, as if from the effects of a distant explosion. I think I can hear the glass rattle.

They are coming closer. Thousands of them, knee-deep through the cornfields, the netting hanging in shreds from

147

their helmets, the bayonets drawing their sharp strokes on mist. In a ditch on the outskirts they are already lining up, the clean spades strapped to their backs. In a mass of fallen rubble a Tiger leans drunkenly, disabled, its gun-turret aimed at no one. They are coming. They have passed through the city already like an earthquake or a hundred-foot wave, shells flaring and bursting as the earth opens to receive them, a church roof a red sheet of flame, fragments of flying buttress crashing through it into the aisle below.

And behind them in the cellars the people are already waking to a world of devastation and smoke. A woman's body is trapped under fallen masonry. A small child is screaming, screaming. Then stops screaming abruptly. An old man is already pushing himself out of a ragged opening, rubbing his eyes.

And the woman is still trapped. A head appears in the hole – young, dirty – a soldier's. She can't tell whether he is one of *them*, or one of the others. She doesn't care, even. It is irrelevant. The night has done something to her. She doesn't want to live here. She looks up at him, almost pleading with him to end it. He comes up to her. In a shaft of dusty light from the hole she can just make out his face. He kicks away the bag of flour she is leaning against and she sprawls full-length on the mud floor. When he stamps on her fingers she feels nothing. Then his bayonet enters her belly, just where the pain is.

And yet he is holding her. As she dies. As her child dies. Someone is supporting her head and offering her water. I open my eyes and see the room, a lamp on in the corner. 'Drink this.' I shake my head. I can't . . . Somewhere under me I hear a car starting, running footsteps, voices. And it is a man's arm that supports me, half-carrying me down the steep stairs.

When I wake, Dominique is at my bedside. A high hospital bed in a room. A locker. No flowers. Through the far window, the hoot and shunt of the city traffic. She looks tired. She doesn't say anything for a minute. Then, gruffly, 'Why the devil didn't you tell us?'

'I didn't tell anyone.'

'How are you feeling?'

148

'Fine.' I consider each part of my body in turn and realise that it is the truth. Nothing hurts. I glance towards the half-open door. 'What are they saying?'

'They say you've come to no harm. They want to keep you under observation for one more night. You can come home tomorrow. I'm collecting you after lunch and driving you back.'

I hesitate for a moment. 'Where's Marthe?'

'She was here until this morning. Then, when you were starting to come round, she decided to go home and get some sleep.'

The window is a perfect white rectangle. A stripe of sun falls across the corner of my bed. Suddenly I remember. 'And what about my car? I left it parked in one of those side-streets behind the *Rectorat* building.'

'Don't worry. Robert and I are going to fetch it this after-noon. One of us will drive it back for you.'

I sigh. 'You're so kind. I'm so lucky to be . . .'

She puts out a hand and touches me on the wrist. 'Don't say it.'

'I ought to have told someone. But I think I always knew the baby wasn't . . . she wouldn't . . .'

Dominique is holding my hand. Suddenly the tears start running down my face, plopping on to the front of the white hospital gown they have dressed me in, wetting the clean turn-back of the sheet. 'All I ever wanted was a job, and a child, and to tell Joseph . . .'

'Shh.' She hands me a tissue from a box on the locker. 'In a year or so all this will be past history. There's absolutely no reason why in a year's time you shouldn't have all those things.'

I ring the bell of our old flat and wait for the buzzer before pushing the familiar door open. I catch it first time as it buzzes. Upstairs, Helen is standing at the open inner door. 'Sarah! Great! I thought you were ill.'

'I was.' She leads me through into the main room and I sit down in my old place, a low chair with a view of the yard, the top branches of a scrubby tree. 'But I'm better now.'

'Was it serious?'

'It was quite nasty. Some kind of virus. They were worried it might turn into pneumonia. I even spent a couple of nights in hospital.'

'You poor thing! How awful!' She disappears through a doorway. From the kitchen she calls out to me. 'Remind me whether or not you take sugar.'

When she comes back, she is carrying that old wooden tray. Two glass bowls of tea, that little tumbler with the pattern of clouds and sheep, full of something that looks like orange-juice. Chryssa is just behind her, holding something. I take the bowl between my two hands and sip it slowly. It's good tea.

'Chryssa's got something to show you,' Helen says.

The little girl comes forward shyly and opens her palms. Between them is something that glitters. 'What is it?'

'They did them at school. Acrylic in a mould. Paperweights.'

I peer into the centre of the little clear dome. A tiny beech-leaf, a fragment of broken twig, a little feather. A smooth pink pebble that seems to shine. 'It's beautiful, Chryssa,' I say to her. 'Thank you for showing me.'

The little girl's head is lowered. She doesn't look at me. She closes her hands again carefully over her treasure and dis-appears with it into the bedroom. 'I'm so happy about her,' Helen says.

I watch the little retreating figure. 'Yes.'

'Did I tell you, about the language thing?'

'You mean the French?'

She nods. 'You know she was refusing to speak it at first? Did I ever tell you? She'd gone right into herself at school, not speaking to anyone. And when she got home she wouldn't even talk to me, in any language. I was getting really worried.'

'Yes. You would.'

'And then, quite suddenly – about four days ago, I think it was – one night, when I was up late to finish a book I was reading and she'd already been asleep for hours – do you know what happened?'

'No.'

'She was all sprawled across the bed, out like a light, on my side, and I rolled her over gently to make room. And do you know what she said?'

'No.'

'She called out *"Arrête!"*.'

'In French?'

'In French.'

'And now . . . ?'

'And now suddenly she's quite different – doing things, making things, talking to me nineteen to the dozen – in double Dutch half the time, but who cares? And wanting to have friends in after school. I'm so relieved!'

'I can imagine.'

'Chryssa!' Helen calls through the open door. 'Can you come here a minute?'

The little girl runs back in. I pat my knee and she comes and sits on it. *'Alors, ça va maintenant, l'école?'* I ask her. *'Tu t'amuses bien, il paraît.'*

'Oui.' She pouts in a very French way. She still has the paperweight in her hand. She is turning it over and over so that the pink stone catches the light. I brush a wisp of hair from her eyes. She twists round to look up at me for a moment. Then she smiles.

Helen shows me out. 'You don't need to come down with me, actually,' I tell her. 'I used to live here, didn't they tell you?'

'In this town?'

'In this flat.'

'You mean, this was where you and Joseph . . . ?' She is staring over my head to where a window looks down on to the tree. It is all just the same, the flaking green paint of the landing, the bulbous radiator. Some small dead thing crumpled on itself in a corner where the concierge's cat has dropped it, some small packet of bones and skin and fluff. At first I think it is a rat. Then I see it is the remains of a bird. Down in the courtyard below us someone is kick-starting a motorbike. And for a moment it is another time I see. Bubbles popping slowly in a pan of soup, skin wrinkling against the bowl of a wooden spoon.

'Why?' I asked you.

You rubbed your eyes, as if you were trying to make the world go away. 'I don't want to talk about it.'

I sat down opposite you, my elbows sliding on the worn plastic. 'We've got to talk about it.'

'Why?'

'People do,' I said. Then, 'I can go home and get an abortion.'

You shook your head. 'I can't be held responsible for that either.'

'What can you be held responsible for?'

'Myself.'

'Be responsible, then. Go back to the States, why don't you? Leave me to work it out. It's not such an enormous thing. It happens all the time. I'll be better off on my own.'

You half-smiled at me then. You said slowly, 'Are you sure?'

I stood up and went back to the cooker. I turned the gas on again, stirring the soup gently until the bubbles started to rise.

And then you had gone into the bedroom. After a moment I heard the noise of the Shepherds' Farewell turned up full blast, filling our few narrow rooms and spilling out on to the landing, until there was nowhere left for me to go.

I tread carefully between the half-packed cardboard boxes that litter the upstairs landing and find my way downstairs. The sitting-room is scarcely any better, the sofa sagging under its pile of books, a white wicker armchair draped with hastily folded clothes. Everything smells of woodsmoke. When I take it all out in some other place, I shall suddenly remember. I shall suddenly see it all clearly, the small windows set in these thick stone walls, the smoked glass of the cast-iron door of the stove with its charred scribble of pine- and birch-sap, the orange roar of the flames.

Under the big mirror of the *armoire*, in a drawer I've never thought to open until now, I find a whole bag stuffed full of junk. It must have been left by Cara and Henry. I up-end the carrier-bag and tip everything out at my feet. Stacking plastic cups in garish primary colours. Board-books, their corners chewed and fraying. A baby's soft hair-brush. Folded Babygros, the nap worn transparent at the toes. I find myself smiling, remembering Josh as he was at 0–3 months, at 3–6. Perhaps one of these days I shall go and see them all.

I stuff whole piles of old photocopies into plastic bags, to be taken to the dump. Then I think better of it and save a single copy of each. Someone might be able to make use of something. Perhaps Helen? I slip them into a light-weight folder. 'Any of these any good to you?' I write two other letters. I address the envelopes carefully. Marthe. Lervain. I drag my two suitcases out from under the bed. The metal trunk on the upstairs landing is already almost full.

I wash my hands and go out on to the gravel. It is a clear, sharp morning. The triangle of grass under the bedroom window is white with frost. When Dominique opens the door to me a breath of warmth blows against my face. She pulls me in and shuts the door. 'Are you almost ready now?'

'Almost.'

'Do you need any help? Is there a load of rubbish to be got rid of?'

'I . . . No, not really. I managed to deal with most of it while I still had the car. But thanks.'

She waves her hands at me in mock exasperation. 'Why do I even ask?! Look, as soon as you've got your things together, the stuff we're storing for you, just tell us. Will you, Sarah? Can I trust you to do that?'

'Yes.'

'You really shouldn't be lifting anything heavy.'

'I know.'

'And how are you feeling?' She rocks back on her heels. 'How's morale?'

'Fine.'

She peers down at me. 'Are you sure?'

'The only thing that makes me a bit sad is not to have seen this place in summer. I keep trying to imagine what it must be like.'

'It gets hot,' she says. 'The grandchildren usually come and visit us. I'm always tripping over their bits and pieces in the grass. The ducks get a bit overexcited sometimes. And flies.'

'Flies?'

'From the cows. They're so close.'

Through the low window on the other side of her kitchen I can see only an empty field. 'They are?'

'Anyway. . . You'll see it, when you come back.'

'If I come back.'

'You'd better come back! Why are we storing your stuff if you've got no intention of ever taking it off our hands?' She

153

pats my shoulder in a friendly sort of way. She doesn't care really.

'I came to ask if I could use your phone again,' I tell her.

'Go ahead.'

I go into the hall. She closes the door behind me discreetly. I hear her turn on the radio suddenly, quite loud, a gabble of French voices, laughter. Then a man's voice singing a sentimental song. I search through the directory for the number I want.

'Allô, Letour Voyages.'

'I'd like to reserve a plane ticket.'

'Yes?'

'From Paris.'

'Destination?'

My voice is quite steady. 'The United States,' I say. 'Boston. As soon as you can find a seat. I've just got to have time to get from here to Paris by train.'

'Why don't you let me push that?' Marthe comes up behind me and takes the guide-rail of the trolley out of my hands.

'I didn't expect to see you here,' I say.

'Why not? You told me you were leaving. All I had to do was ring Dominique for the exact time.'

'But . . .' My own objection escapes me. We trundle up the platform in silence. Almost at the far end she stops and swings the trolley round to face the tracks. 'Marthe . . .' I say.

'Mm?' She has let go of the trolley. She gets a packet of Gauloises out of her pocket and bends to light one, her hand shaking in the light of the flame.

I turn my head away from the smoke. 'Why did you come back?'

'This morning?'

'No. The other night. What made you come back and find me?'

'Oh . . .' She takes a drag and taps with her finger as if to dislodge an invisible pencil of ash. 'Your handbag. You left it in my car. And it had all your things in it – money, cards, glasses, photos . . . What could I do?'

'Only one photo,' I say.

She throws the cigarette down before it is finished and

154

stamps it out on the platform. When she moves her foot I see that the butt is pressed almost perfectly flat.

'I didn't know you smoked.'

She opens her mouth to say something, and thinks better of it. Finally she says, 'We should exchange addresses, at least.'

'I don't know where I'll be, exactly. But you can probably reach me with this.' I scribble out your Boston address and hand it to her. 'Not much point giving me yours, though.'

'What do you mean?'

'Well, aren't you going somewhere else?'

'Why should I be?'

'To get away from the terrible teachers,' I say. 'I thought . . .'

She doesn't answer. The train is gliding slowly in now, doors crashing back, metal on metal. She bends to put her weight behind the trolley as she wheels it to the end of the nearest queue. We wait as the incoming passengers step down. Finally I am pulling myself in and bending low to take the cases as she passes them in to me. As I grasp the second one she leans in and gives me a quick, awkward hug. 'Why should I bother to leave, now all the terrible teachers have gone?'

I pull back into the shadows of the corridor before I can see her start to cry.